P9-DGW-654

With
Secrets
to Keep

Rose Levit

SHOE TREE PRESS
WHITE HALL, VIRGINIA

Published by Shoe Tree Press, an imprint of
Betterway Publications, Inc.
P.O. Box 219
Crozet, VA 22932
(804) 823-5661

Cover design and photograph by Susan Riley
Typography by Park Lane Associates

Levit, Rose
    With secrets to keep / Rose Levit.
        p. cm.
    Summary: Thirteen-year-old Adrianna, overweight and dreamy, is
helped at school when she becomes friends with popular Jenny, but
her disturbing home life with an abusive father brings problems less
easily solved.
    ISBN 1-55870-197-4
    [1. Family problems--Fiction. 2. Schools--Fiction.
3. Friendship--Fiction.] I. Title.
PZ7.L5797Wi 1991
[Fic]--dc20   90-20947
                                                            CIP
                                                             AC

Printed in the United States of America
0 9 8 7 6 5 4 3 2 1

With love —
for Max and Jana

Chapter 1

"Adrianna Espirikos!" His voice rasped with impatience. "Late again! What's your excuse this time?"

Adrianna stopped short in the doorway and shifted her arm-load of books. One fell, and she knelt to retrieve it while a titter ran through the classroom. "Sorry, Mr. Mitchell. I couldn't get my locker open. The lock. It jammed . . ." Her voice trailed to a whisper. Flushing as she felt thirty pairs of eyes fixed on her, she made her way to her desk, dropped her books on the floor, and slumped into a chair. She rummaged in her purse and found a pencil, then opened her notebook and settled back, resigned to the boredom of this fifth period Science class.

Mr. Mitchell sighed. "Well, let's get on with it," he said. "Yesterday I asked you to read the third chapter in your text-book. How many of you did?"

Adrianna glanced around and saw a scattering of upraised hands. She kept her own down and nervously fingered the wool fuzz of her cardigan sweater.

Mr. Mitchell sighed again. "The film we're about to see," he said, "is on the human reproductive system. It goes with that chapter."

Adrianna riffled through the pages of her book. She found the third chapter and gazed at the vivid illustrations of male and female anatomies. She felt chilled. She closed her book with a shiver and tried to shut out the drone of Mr. Mitchell's voice as he said, "Tomorrow, we'll have a quiz."

A girl's voice asked. "A quiz? On what?"

"On the film, stupid," a boy answered while others snickered.

Volunteer hands pulled the window curtains to darken the

the room, dimming the afternoon glare of bright California sun-shine. Adrianna stared at the diagrams on the screen and listen-ed to the narrator's description of the female reproductive system. She squirmed. What was new about this? She had seen films like this every year since fifth grade until now in this eighth grade life-science class.

But soon the film focused on a larger-than-life picture of male anatomy. She shuddered. Nausea surged up from her stomach, and she tasted again the pizza she had devoured at lunchtime today; the flavors of sausage and cheese were sour in her mouth now. Her head tightened. Her heart pounded, and a lump grew in her throat. She knew an eruption was coming. Prodded by memories of other times when her stomach had be-trayed her, she clamped a hand to her mouth, snatched up her purse, and fled from the room. Mr. Mitchell, seated beside his projector, watched her and frowned.

In the safety of the girls' washroom, Adrianna bent over the sink and sloshed water at her face. Her hands dripping, she brushed loose straggles of hair away from her face and swal-lowed hard. She thought of other times like this, times at home when she had heaved and retched while Philomene, her older sister, stood by, and their mother cried out, "Breathe, Adrianna. Breathe deep! From the toes."

Now, in the washroom, Adrianna groaned between gasps, "Breathe deep. Don't throw up!" And the surges receded. But then came disgust. Sick again! Why? What was wrong with her? No one else she knew threw up like this. She mopped the sweat from her forehead and wondered if today's blistering heat had made her feel sick. And then she remembered last night and the candies she had eaten when she couldn't sleep.

She had been awakened by noises, sounds that came through the wall from Philomene's room, clicks of a door opening and shutting, and muffled voices, Philomene's and Papa's, saying words Adrianna couldn't understand, words that were only a murmur. Roused from sleep, she wondered if Frederika, her little sister who slept in the bed beside hers, had been awakened too. But no sound came from that bed, and in the dark Adrianna saw nothing. She whispered Frederika's name. No answer. With a sudden deep void in her stomach, she groped in the drawer of her bedside table for a box of chocolate covered cherries she kept hidden there. She ate one, and its soft creamy sweetness soothed the unrest in her stomach. She felt comforted, but wondered about those noises. Did she dream or imagine them? And what about other times when sounds through the wall had awakened her? Had she imagined those too?

Wide awake as she wondered, she nibbled on another candy. Then her thoughts drifted to pictures and scenes — wishes and half-dreams — of herself as a famous author, greeted at the airport by reporters and cameramen after a whirlwind tour of promoting her latest novel. The person in her fantasy was a slim, graceful, young woman who was smiling and confident, so different from the shy, dumpy person she knew she really was. Consoled by the pictures in her head, she savored another candy and then another.

She had fallen asleep finally as night turned to morning, but woke with a start — just moments later, it seemed. Bright sunlight streamed through the window and flooded the room. Frederika's bed was empty. Adrianna felt her heart sink. Late for school again! Why hadn't her mother come in to wake her? She jumped out of bed and flung on the clothes she had worn to school yesterday — the same tan cardigan sweater and pleated skirt — too warm for comfort, she knew, in this hot mid-October weather.

With her teeth quickly brushed but her tongue still thick and furry and her long taffy-brown hair pulled tight in a ponytail, she glanced in the bathroom mirror and shrugged at the clouded blue eyes that looked back at her. She collected her books and headed for the front door.

"Breakfast, Adrianna!" Mama had called from the kitchen.

"Why didn't you wake me?" Adrianna called back.

"I try it," her mother answered. "But you shake off my hand. So I let you sleep."

"Oh . . ." Adrianna said, with a sudden recollection of Mama's hand on her shoulder and her own need to sleep on. "It's okay. I have early lunch period. I'll eat then. I've got money for pizza." Already through the door and out of the house, she knew her mother couldn't hear her.

At school now, in the dank cool of the girls' washroom, Adrianna shivered and hugged her sweater. What time was it? She dreaded the bell that would ring soon and signal the break between classes. With doors flying open and students milling in the corridors, she knew her refuge would soon be invaded by throngs of girls, interrupting their own giggles and small talk to look askance at her pale face and pudgy figure.

She had to escape. Tears filled her eyes as she peered into the corridor and saw it was empty. She ventured out and forced herself to stroll past the office and the carved redwood sign that welcomed visitors to Middleton's Creekside Junior High School.

She ran. And panted. And walked. And ran again until she reached home. When she opened the door and stumbled in, she found her mother in the kitchen. Frederika, home after her morning in kindergarten, sat at the table and crooned a song to herself while she scrawled in her coloring book. Mama, her hands dripping, turned from the sink when Adrianna burst in.

"I was sick!" Adrianna cried. "I started to throw up in class."

Frederika returned to her coloring. Mama shook her head, wiped her hands on her apron, and opened her arms.

✳

After a steaming bowlful of Mama's lemon-chicken soup, Adrianna lay on the couch and watched television. But tears remained near. She opened her book; it was a story about a girl named Tina who was slim and vivacious, popular with her classmates in high school, but always in trouble with her teachers. Adrianna had enjoyed reading it yesterday, but today her own troubles interfered. She turned the book over and tried to blank her mind through watching television.

But her sister distracted her. Sprawled on the floor, Frederika played with her dolls, her voice shrill over the drama on television. "No! You did that all wrong!" she scolded them. "Don't you know any better?"

The front door slammed. Adrianna winced, and Frederika fell silent. Their father was home.

Mama came from the kitchen. With an apron over her house-dress and a wooden spoon in her hand, she stood, short and stocky, her dark hair frizzed around her face. "Home already?" she said and turned down the television.

"We finished the job," Papa said gruffly. "I let the men off early." He stood in the entry and shuffled through letters he had taken from the mailbox.

Adrianna glanced sideways at her father. Tall and robust, his muscles bulging under the short-sleeved cotton shirt that he wore with his work pants today, Papa — as he stood there right now — looked heavy, almost clumsy. Yet Adrianna knew that when he moved, he was smooth, even graceful and light on his feet. Time and again, his swiftness of movement surprised her. It seemed so at odds with his big burly body and his rough way of talking. Often, she found herself thinking that he moved like a cat, a powerful one, a lion or tiger.

He stopped shuffling through his mail when he saw Adrianna and asked, "Why is she home?"

Mama's answer was quick. "She is sick. She throws up."

"Again?" Papa's face darkened. He strode to the kitchen, tossed his mail on the table, then settled into a chair and bent over to unlace his work shoes.

Frederika, watching him, scrambled to her feet and ran to the hall closet. She was back in an instant with his slippers, brown felt, lined with soft sheepskin. "Here, Papa," she said.

"Good girl." He reached into his pocket and pulled out a shiny new quarter. "I saved this for you." He smiled and patted her smooth brown braids. "Kindergarten was good?" he asked.

Frederika beamed. "Yep. We played horses today. And I spelled my name right." Back with her dolls, she played without making a sound.

The telephone rang, and Mama answered. "Yes . . . ? She is here. Since two hours." Her face somber, she stared at the spoon in her hand and said, "My husband is here. You talk to him."

Adrianna half-rose from the couch. She felt her stomach knot when Mama said, "Anthony, the school — they say Adrianna does wrong."

Papa snatched the phone from her, then listened and scowled. "What?" he said, stroking his dark bristly mustache. "Tomorrow morning? All right." He slammed the phone down and turned to Adrianna. "Why do you make trouble? Always, you don't stay in school. What is this — you run home all the time?"

Mama protested. "Anthony, she is sick."

He turned on her. "Sick! You baby her! You should send her right back."

Mama looked down.

Papa grumbled. "Now I have to take time from the job and go there tomorrow. Tomorrow! I've got a new job to start. To lay a foundation."

"You don't have to come with me." Adrianna tried to keep her voice steady. "Mama could come."

"No. I'll take you. The men can start without me."

Mama's shoulders drooped. She looked from Adrianna to Papa and murmured, "Next time I send her right back."

"What's up?" It was Philomene, home from school. No one had

heard her come in. She dropped her books on the table and ran her fingers through her dark curly hair. "What a day! Too hot for October. I'm melting. And I'm loaded with homework."

With smooth olive skin and startling green eyes, Philomene was slender and graceful. She was beautiful, Adrianna thought, her appearance all that Adrianna could wish for herself. The day suddenly brightened, and she felt cheerful again. She knew that Philomene would understand. "I was sick in school," she said. "I had to come home."

Her father exploded. "Sick! What is this sick! All the time sick!" He shook his fist in her face.

Adrianna shrank. Was he going to hit her? Speechless, she felt herself shriveling into a tiny, helpless self in her big thirteen-year-old body.

"Don't, Papa. Don't hit her." Philomene flashed a smile at him and brushed her hand lightly over his shirt sleeve. Then she said to her sister. "Come on, Adrianna — grow up! You're too old for this stuff. You'll be in high school next year. They won't let you cut class."

Adrianna's voice quavered. "It'll be different in high school."

"Yeah. Sure it will. So start staying in school now." Philomene turned back to Papa. "What's the big fuss? She didn't miss that much. She won't do it again."

Papa smiled, and Adrianna sighed with relief. This time, at least, she was safe.

Chapter 2

Early the next morning, Papa drove his white Cadillac up the school driveway and parked in the red zone. Adrianna started to say, "There's no parking here." But she clamped her mouth shut and moved toward the office on feet like lead weights, with her father's hand at her elbow propelling her there.

The secretary smiled at her. "Hello, Adrianna," she said. "And Mr. Espirikos — ?"

He nodded, his face grim.

"Please go in. Mrs. Feldman expects you."

In the counselor's office, Adrianna slouched in a chair, then adjusted her tan sweater and folded her hands over the book in her lap while Mrs. Feldman said, "I'm glad to meet you, Mr. Espirikos. I'm Adrianna's counselor."

"Why does she need a counselor?"

"Mostly so she'll take the right courses. But sometimes for other things too." The smile on Mrs. Feldman's face faded. "Right now, I'm concerned about Adrianna's attendance. You know, the law in California says she must come to school every day. No unexcused absences. And not so much tardiness."

"Yes — ?"

Adrianna wondered if Papa was agreeing or questioning. She studied her fingers and poked at a cuticle, pushing it back from the base of her thumbnail. She wished Papa would let her wear nail polish. Lots of girls her age did. They wore make-up too — lip gloss and blusher, sometimes mascara and eye shadow. But he wouldn't even let Philomene do that, and she was a junior in high school. Why was he so strict? She focused her thoughts on the book in her lap, the one about Tina. Sixteen in the story,

Tina would never sit still and let people discuss her. She would rise up and say, "You must excuse me. I have other things to do." And with that, she would sail from the room. Slim and pretty in the story, Tina was outrageously assertive, and Adrianna yearned to be like her.

"So — ?" Her father's brusque voice interrupted her thoughts.

"So let's talk about Adrianna's school work. And her attendance."

Papa said nothing.

"She's not doing well."

"Oh — ?"

"She's way behind in her work. I checked with her teachers."

Adrianna protested. "Not in English."

Mrs. Feldman agreed. "No, not in English. But in math and science."

"Math and science," Adrianna said. "I hate them."

Papa frowned, but Mrs. Feldman went on. "I talked to Miss Larsen. She says you keep cutting her gym class."

What could Adrianna say? She knew this was true.

Her father defended her. "She's a good reader. At home all the time, she sits with her nose in a book."

"Yes, and her English teacher says she writes beautiful poetry. But why is she absent so much?"

"You should ask her, not me."

They both turned to her, and Adrianna tried to explain. "Sometimes I get sick. My head hurts. My stomach gets upset."

"How about yesterday?" Mrs. Feldman asked. "You skipped first period entirely. Then after lunch you were late to your science class. And you caused a disturbance. And ran out."

Adrianna shifted the book in her lap and mumbled, "I overslept. Then after lunch my locker jammed. And I didn't like the film." Her head throbbed.

"What about the film? I don't understand. Can you tell me?"

Adrianna shook her head. How could she? She didn't under-

14

stand it herself. She only knew that watching it made her feel awful, even though she'd seen others like it before and knew everything in it. Well, maybe not everything. But almost.

Mrs. Feldman studied Adrianna's face and asked, "Have you been to a doctor lately?"

Papa looked past Adrianna and answered for her. "Sure. Just last month. My wife took her."

"And — ?"

"He could find nothing. Not in any of his tests. Nothing wrong."

"Oh — ?"

"She's too fat. You can see for yourself."

Mrs. Feldman nodded.

Papa gave a short laugh. "She was so skinny when she was little. Now look at her."

"What else did the doctor say?"

"He said she weighs too much."

"Anything else?"

"He says girls of her age cry a lot. But they get over it. And she should go to school every day."

"Yes, she should," Mrs. Feldman said. "Adrianna, please, will you try?"

Tears overflowed and splashed on Adrianna's hands, dampening the cover of her book. "I don't know," she whispered.

"What do you mean, you don't know?" Papa's voice rose.

"School can be fun, you know," Mrs. Feldman said hastily.

Adrianna thought back to the times when school had been fun, times when she had lots of friends and met them at the bike rack every morning before walking to class.

As if reading her thoughts, Mrs. Feldman said, "You attended Woodland School before you came here . . ."

"Yes."

"And most of the kids at that elementary school went to the other junior high. Too bad the attendance boundary cut right through your neighborhood."

15

"My friend, Sarah . . ." Adrianna said, "she was my best friend at Woodland."

"Was that Sarah Benson?" Mrs. Feldman asked.

Adrianna nodded. "She came here to Creekside. When I did. But then she moved away."

"I know." Mrs. Feldman's voice sounded sympathetic. "It was so sudden — the way her father was transferred last year. To Denver, wasn't it?"

Adrianna looked down. Flooded by feelings of loss and loneliness, she didn't trust herself to speak.

"But you can make other friends."

Adrianna sat mute.

Mrs. Feldman persisted. "How about clubs? That's a good way to make friends. There's one you might like. A writing club. It meets after school. Miss Delricco — "

Papa interrupted. "No. Not after school. Adrianna should come home after school."

"But — "

He interrupted again. "I can't sit here all day. I have work to do. Adrianna, you stay now. You hear me?" He stood and gave a curt nod, then turned and strode from the room. They looked at his empty chair. His presence had filled the room; now the room seemed empty too.

"Adrianna, is there something you want to tell me?" Mrs. Feldman sounded troubled.

"Well . . ." Adrianna said, then stopped. She felt drawn to this woman whom she hardly knew. But what could she tell her? What could she say about Papa's anger, his rages? How could she put into words the terror and guilt that she felt when she offended him? She shook her head and said nothing while the tears dried in streaks on her face.

Mrs. Feldman sighed. "It's getting late," she said. "Third period already. What class do you have now?"

"English. Miss Delricco."

"You'll need a pass. I'll write one for you."

Adrianna took it and dragged herself from the office and through empty corridors to Miss Delricco's room. Stifling her urge to run home, she cracked the door open and peered in. Class was in session. She took a deep breath, then walked in, handed the teacher her pass, and found a seat. The class buzzed.

Miss Delricco walked back to the chalkboard and picked up the thread of her lesson. "Take this subject — the wind. Who can give it a strong predicate?"

No one raised a hand.

"No volunteers?" Miss Delricco said cheerfully. "Okay — we'll take turns around the room."

Everyone groaned.

"Well, we could have everyone write a paper," she said, her voice still cheerful. "Let's do that."

"Hey, no!" Pete Lindstrom called out. "It's better out loud."

Miss Delricco smiled. "I think so too. Who'll start?"

Teresa Valdez spoke up. "... whispered softly," she said hesitantly.

"Yes. But say the whole sentence."

"The wind whispered softly."

"Good. Jenny, you're next."

"The wind played with the leaves." Jenny's answer was quick. She was like that, Adrianna thought. Quick, and with always the right answer. Sometimes in class or when they said brief hellos at their lockers, Adrianna wished they could be friends, real friends. But she knew that couldn't be. With all the friends Jenny Harris had, what chance was there for Adrianna?

Miss Delricco's voice penetrated Adrianna's thoughts. "I like that sentence, Jenny. Pete, now."

On and on they went. As other voices took turns, Adrianna relaxed and let their words pour over her.

"Adrianna — ?" It was her turn.

Startled, she looked up; she had lost track again. She reached

17

inside and pulled out the first words that came to her. ". . . shrieked," she said. "The wind shrieked at the shrouded sky."

Chapter 3

Adrianna walked slowly down Oak Street. School was out for the day, but she had no books to carry, no homework to do. It was Halloween.

She knew that some kids were going to parties tonight. She'd heard them talking in class and at their lockers. But she wasn't; no one had invited her. As if Papa would let her go, even if they had. No, she would take Frederika trick-or-treating tonight; she had promised.

Bikers wheeled past her. They pedaled with care through the street's flow of traffic; at least most of them did. But some didn't. They rode against traffic, playing bike tag, darting between cars. Adrianna watched with disapproval and envy.

She thought back to the times when she rode her bike to school — parking and locking it in the bike rack, meeting her friends, standing and talking until the bell rang for class. Adrianna missed riding her bike; she missed her friends too. But most of all she missed Sarah. She remembered the fun they had then and smiled wistfully.

In those days at Woodland, Sarah was the leader, always laughing and joking, while Adrianna followed. If Sarah were here at Creekside, school might still be fun. Other girls might still be friendly. Walking home now, Adrianna thought about other girls that she knew. Friendly when Sarah was here, they avoided Adrianna now. They hung out with different friends and barely gave her a nod. Why? Was it something she had done? She felt so alone, almost like an outcast.

And boys. Most girls Adrianna's age went to parties and movies with boys, to school dances and games. Last year, she and

and Sarah were invited. And Sarah went, but Papa never allowed Adrianna to go. Now no one invited her, and most boys ignored her.

But some didn't. Some teased and ridiculed her. And with Sarah gone, there was no one she could turn to. Not even Philomene who was busy in high school and had her own friends.

Adrianna eyed the bikers who passed, and pictured her own bike, parked in the garage at home. She no longer rode it to school. When she tried it at home a few weeks ago, Philomene had laughed. "You look silly on it. It's too small for you. You need a new one."

Well, Adrianna thought, perhaps Papa would buy her a new one some day. A ten-speed. But she didn't think she'd ride even a new one to school. She might look silly on it too.

"Hey!" She heard raucous voices. "There's Addie! Fat Addie!"

Her heart sank. She had hoped to avoid the teasers today. But here they came, riding three abreast, Leland Baxter and two of his buddies. This time she didn't even know the other two, but she knew Leland from way back in grade school. A tormentor then as now, always loud, forever in trouble with teachers, and always acting as if he hated her.

"What a blimp!"

"Naw, that's no blimp. That's a pig. Hey, Addie! Oink, oink!"

"Man! You guys got it all wrong. That's a duck. See it waddle! Hey, Addie — let's hear you quack. Let's hear it in Greek."

Adrianna's cheeks burned. Pulling the soft wool of her sweater around her, she fixed an expression of disdain on her face and marched on. She tried to ignore them.

It worked. This time, ignoring them worked. They sped on. Filled with relief, she stepped up her pace. Better hurry, she thought. She knew that Frederika was waiting at home for help with a costume they'd planned, a bride costume from a curtain and a white satin petticoat.

"Hi, Adrianna." She heard another voice, a friendly one this time. She looked up to see Jenny Harris race by on a silver and green ten-speed. Straight and swift in her riding, Jenny was gone before Adrianna could answer. Adrianna's eyes followed her.

✳

In the driveway at home, she saw Papa's car. He was back from work early again. She sighed and thought of the snack that she wanted, a tall glass of milk and a thick slice of cake. Now she'd have to settle for an apple. She opened the front door, unlocked as always, and heard her father's voice, loud and angry.

He was pacing back and forth in the kitchen and glaring at Philomene while Mama sat at the table, her eyes down, her hands peeling potatoes. A stew, fragrant with onions and garlic, simmered on the stove.

"No!" Papa shouted. "I say no! Not a party with boys."

Philomene stood still and answered. "I'm going. I told you last week. And you said maybe. And I made plans."

"You said something like that? No, I don't remember."

"I heard her say . . ." Mama said hesitantly.

He turned on her. "You keep out of this. What do you know about such a party? I know what they do."

Mama bent over her work.

"Papa, we're not going to do anything. It's just that we're too old to go trick-or-treating. So there's this boy — Roger — and he invited some kids over. To answer the door. And give the little kids candy."

"And what else?"

"I don't know. Maybe play records."

"This Roger — do I know him?"

"How could you? He's just a boy in my history class."

"Who else will be there?"

"Just some other kids — "

21

"Ah-ha!" Papa interrupted. "How do you know some others will be there? These boys — you cannot trust them."

Quiet for a moment, Philomene stared at him, her green eyes wide open and dark with anger. Then she cried, "Oh, you! You're not fair!" She turned and stormed down the hall. She slammed her bedroom door shut, and soon from that room they heard bedlam break loose. Adrianna could picture her sister pounding the wall and kicking it. It had happened before, other times when she couldn't get her way. Adrianna stood. Mama sat. Sobs, unabated, rang through the house.

Adrianna sighed. No snack today. Not even an apple. "Where's Freddie?" she asked.

"In your bedroom," Mama answered. "She waits there for you."

Adrianna glanced toward the half-open door of the room she shared with Frederika. "Okay, I'll help her. Then I'll lie down. My head hurts."

In their room, Frederika ignored the sounds from Philomene's room. "Addie, here's the curtain. Mama washed it. And here's a headband. Will you sew it on?"

"Yes." Adrianna tried to sound cheerful. "I'll get a needle and thread. And where's the petticoat?"

"Mama said she'd press it. But then Papa came home. And Philomene started fighting with him."

"Wait here." Adrianna went out and left Frederika with the window curtain that would soon be her veil.

In the kitchen, Mama scraped carrots under fast running water. Papa sat at the table, his head in his hands, his face hidden.

Adrianna spoke to her mother's back. "I need a needle and white thread. And where's the petticoat?"

Mama turned and pointed. "There. Nice and damp for the iron."

Adrianna set up the board and plugged in the iron. She pressed the white satin, Philomene's petticoat from an old party dress. Just right for a bride costume. The satin shone.

The sound of sobbing grew louder. All at once, Papa shoved his chair back, strode down the hall, and flung Philomene's door open. "All right!" he shouted. "I'll let you go! But be home by ten."

Like Mama's spigot of fast-running water, the sobs were turned off in an instant, and Philomene flew from her room. "Thank you! Oh, thank you, Papa!"

"By ten. You hear me?"

"Yes. Thank you."

Adrianna caught sight of her father standing in the hallway. He reached out and caught Philomene, folding her in his arms and hugging her tight. Adrianna's stomach knotted. She swallowed hard and looked at her mother. Had she seen? But Mama still stood at the sink, rinsing her potatoes and carrots. Adrianna looked down at the last careful touch of the iron on white satin while Mama moved to the stove with her vegetables and sliced them into the stew.

Chapter 4

Back from their Halloween expedition, Frederika hoisted her pillowcase sack, filled with candy, up to the kitchen table. "That costume was no good," she complained. "My dress was too long. I kept tripping. We should've made a pirate costume."

"Next time," Adrianna said. "Go to bed now."

"I want some candy."

"One piece. Save the rest for later."

"Okay." Frederika pulled a licorice whip from her sack and trudged off to bed.

Adrianna glanced toward the bedroom at the end of the hallway, the room shared by their parents. That door was closed. Mama must have gone to bed early. She peeked into the living room and saw Papa sunk in his easy chair; he was still watching television. No sign of Philomene.

"We're home, Papa," she called. "Freddie got lots of candy."

"So, all right. Go to bed." He didn't turn from the television.

Adrianna searched the refrigerator and poured a tall glass of milk for herself, then rummaged in Frederika's sack for a candy bar. She found one and pulled its silver foil wrapper away. She took small nibbling bites of the chocolate and nuts, enjoying the sweetness, washing it all down with milk.

She thought back over the day. At school in her English class, they had written poems about animals. Some kids wrote about imaginary creatures, and everyone laughed when they read their work aloud. But she wrote about Misty, her cat when she was just a small girl, not much older than Frederika was now. Adrianna had loved that plume-tailed gray cat. And Misty loved her in return, Adrianna was sure; he always came when she called. But one summer when Papa took the family on a visit to Greece, she had to leave Misty with a neighbor at home. And while they were gone, he ran away. Just vanished completely one day, the neighbor said when they came back from their trip. Stricken, Adrianna and Mama had searched the neighborhood. But they never found him. He never came back. Today, Adrianna read her poem to the class. She was nervous, and her voice trembled, but no one laughed. Later, in the school corridor, Jenny Harris caught up with her and told her how much she liked the poem. So that was one good part of this day.

And today's Halloween excursion through the neighborhood had been good. No one made fun of Adrianna in her loose-fitting tan sweater and baggy blue jeans as she trailed after the little girl dressed like a bride with dirty white tennis shoes trampling the hem of her gown.

But the argument between Philomene and Papa had been bad. And where was Philomene now? Adrianna eyed the clock on the kitchen wall and called, "I'm going to bed now, Papa."

He didn't answer. She rinsed her glass clean and closed Frederika's sack. With so many treats, Freddie would surely not miss one candy bar. She glanced at the clock again; it was only nine-thirty.

In their bedroom, Frederika was sound asleep. Adrianna yawned and climbed into bed, then pulled the blanket up to her chin and plunged deep into sleep.

❋

Asleep. Had she been asleep long? Jolted awake, Adrianna squinted at her clock radio, a present last year from Papa. The clock face glowed green in the dark; it was past midnight and her father's voice, echoing down the hallway from the kitchen, had awakened her. "It's midnight! I told you to be home by ten."

Adrianna heard her sister's voice. "I'm sorry. The time got away from me." Philomene's words were meek, her tone mild.

26

"What did you do at this party?"

"Nothing."

"What is that — nothing?"

"We answered the door. And gave treats to the little kids."

"Oh — ?"

"Yes."

"The little kids. They came all this time? Up till midnight?" Sarcasm tinged Papa's voice.

"Well, no. But Roger's mom said we could make popcorn. So we did."

"What else did you do there?"

"We drank cokes and played records."

"And danced — ?"

"Yeah. We danced." Now Philomene sounded sullen.

"Go to bed!" Papa said sharply. "And don't ask me again to go out on a school night."

No answer. But soon a door slammed and sent tremors through the wall from Philomene's room. Frederika slept on, but Adrianna was wide awake now, awake and strung tight, as she lay in the dark and wondered if Mama had heard the argument. She stared at the ceiling and wished she could empty all thoughts from her head so she could go back to sleep. Tomorrow she had to get up early. Since their meeting with Mrs. Feldman, Papa was adamant; she couldn't miss school or be late anymore.

In need of comfort, she reached for a fresh box of chocolates she had hidden in her drawer. Just one candy tonight. She wanted to cut down since her last bout of sickness at school. She sucked on a chocolate, then mashed it in her mouth and relished its taste before she summoned her will power and slid the drawer shut.

She plumped up her pillow and settled down to sleep, but soon she heard a door creak; it was Philomene's. And in the hushed stillness, she heard the sound of her father's voice. Adrianna had heard it before, other times like this — his voice, rough but not harsh, the words muffled and urgent. Never a sound from Philomene. Adrianna crept from her bed. She pulled her hair back and plastered her ear to the wall, but she could hear nothing. Yet he was still there, she was certain. What was he doing? Was he sleeping in Philomene's room?

One night — a long time ago, years before Freddie was born — Adrianna had gone to bed crying, alone in her room. Perhaps she had done something wrong — she couldn't recall — and Papa in his rage had hit her so hard that her ears rang. She remembered feeling miserable and crying for hours until he came to her room and wrapped his arms around her. He said he still loved her and held her close. That night he fell asleep on her bed, and they slept together that way until morning.

In those days, she knew Papa loved her. Although he sometimes hit her, they always made up. But it wasn't that way anymore. Now he was angry so often, and he never came in to comfort her. He seemed to stay angry forever.

Yet he made up with Philomene. Adrianna heard him when he went into that room — sometimes after an argument, sometimes after nothing that seemed like a reason. It bothered her. It didn't seem right. But what could be wrong? Was she jealous? Did she wish Papa would be nice to her too? She didn't know. She found herself trembling.

Kneeling by the wall, she lost track of time and dozed until suddenly Philomene's door opened and shut; the sound woke her. She heard a light tread of footsteps down the hall. It was quiet in Philomene's room. Chilled, her teeth chattering, Adrianna slipped back to her bed; exhausted, she fell asleep.

Chapter 5

November. Wind-driven rain from the Pacific swept like a gale over northern California and drenched Middleton. Safe at home, Adrianna sat in the living room with Papa and Frederika while in the kitchen Mama prepared Sunday dinner, and Philomene, complaining about homework, stayed in her room.

Papa and Frederika sat together in his big armchair and watched television — a program of figure skaters in bright satin costumes streaking splashes of crimson and blue on the screen as their skates skimmed over the ice. But Adrianna sat by the fire and stared at the flames until — feeling dazzled, her eyes almost scorched — she shifted her gaze to the cool gray of the fireplace wall.

That wall was massive; crag-faced, it rose to the high beams of the ceiling and extended the full length of the living room. Papa had built that wall himself of rocks quarried nearby in Sonoma. And his fireplace drew well; he often boasted about that. Its flames danced over the soot-blackened grate, and every wisp of smoke went up the flue.

In fact, Papa had built the entire house. Construction was his business, and he showed his pleasure and pride in it when he told other people of how he had come to this country just ten years ago, and then settled in Middleton, to build his business here and this home for his family. With Mama, he insisted, even argued, that life here was better than it could be in Greece. Silence was Mama's only response, but Adrianna could tell from the look on her face that she didn't agree.

Knowing how much Mama missed her family in Greece, Adrianna sometimes tried to remember her own early years there. But she couldn't. Her childhood memories began here; this was her home. And Philomene, who perhaps recalled more, said little; she seldom listened when Mama reminisced. What Adrianna did clearly remember of Greece was their visit to her grandfather's house in Epirus that long-ago summer when she was six. She had loved being there, and she understood her mother's homesickness.

Now feeling warm and secure by the fire, Adrianna dreamily thought about that visit while outside the wind whistled, rain pelted the windows, and creaking eucalyptus branches scraped on the roof. She sniffed appreciatively at the aroma of roast lamb that drifted from the kitchen and stole a quick glance at her father. He was smiling at the skaters on television.

"Play cards with me, Addie." Frederika's voice interrupted her thoughts. "I'm tired of watching."

"What game?"

"War. I'll get the cards." Frederika scrambled out of Papa's chair.

"War! That's boring."

"But I like it. Please . . ."

"Well — okay." Adrianna knew she could let her thoughts wander while she played this game with her sister. She pulled thick velvet cushions from the couch to the floor, and they sat by the fire and played. Frederika slapped her cards down and crowed when she scooped up Adrianna's. Soon her winnings were high.

From his chair by the television, Papa scolded, "Be quiet, Frederika. You make too much noise."

"Adrianna!" Mama called from the kitchen. "Come. Set the table."

"I'm coming." Adrianna eyed Frederika's stack of cards. "You won. You got the most cards."

"I won! Papa, I beat Adrianna. Will you play with me now?"

"Wait for the program to end. Come, sit on my lap."

In the kitchen, Adrianna spread a white linen cloth on the table; Mama had embroidered a green leafy pattern in fine silken stitches on it years ago when she was a young girl in Greece. Adrianna smoothed it now and took pleasure in its beauty. Blue and white plates, gleaming silver for Sunday — she set them out quickly before asking her mother, "How was church today?"

"Church? It was good." Mama looked up from the roast she was basting. A smile brightened her face, but she said nothing more.

She had gone to church early this morning. Seeing the dark clouds that heralded today's storm, she had tied a black scarf over her short permanent-waved curls, wrapped herself in her coat, and walked the long blocks to church. Other Sundays, Adrianna went with her. And sometimes Frederika, sleepy and protesting, came too. But lately Mama didn't ask them to come — and more and more often they stayed home with Papa and Philomene, sleeping late and waking to the fragrance of breakfast kept warm in the oven while she went to church alone.

Sometimes Adrianna caught herself thinking that if only Mama looked prettier, more like other mothers in Middleton, she might still enjoy going to church with her. Once, months ago, she had asked, "Mama, why do you wear that black dress all the time? You could wear your pretty flowered dress to church."

But her mother pressed her lips in a thin tight line and shook her head as if to say, "Black is for church. I know what is right."

Adrianna felt guilty, ashamed of her thoughts, as she set the table now. Did Mama know how she felt? But her mother's face, as she washed her hands and took off her apron, told her nothing. Wondering about Mama's thoughts, Adrianna suddenly yearned to talk to her about other things, perhaps even about Papa and Philomene. Did she ever hear noises at night? Did she know that sometimes Papa stayed a long time in Philomene's

31

room? Adrianna wanted her mother to laugh and say that of course she knew about it, and certainly it was all right for Papa to go into Philomene's room and patch up his quarrel with her.

"Mama . . ." she said hesitantly, "can I ask you something?"

"Yes — ?"

"Why do you go to sleep so early? Why don't you stay up and keep Papa company?" Once out, her words sounded foolish to her, but they weren't what she had intended to say.

Mama cast a sharp glance at her. "Why — ? Because I work hard. I get tired. So I go to bed."

"I mean . . ."

"We eat now," Mama said. "Anthony! Frederika. Philomene. Come!"

※

At dinner, Papa heaped food on their plates, and Adrianna ate quickly. When she passed her plate back for more, he eyed her with doubt but gave her a second slice of tender roast lamb and another helping of rice. Eating without conversation, they were soon finished; then he pushed himself back from the table and returned to the living room.

"Philomene, Adrianna — clean up now," Mama said.

Philomene protested. "I've got too much homework."

"The dishes first." Seldom did their mother insist; this time she didn't wait for Philomene's answer, but instead followed Papa to the living room.

"I'll clear the table," Adrianna said, "if you'll load the dishwasher, Phil."

"Okay . . . okay," Philomene grumbled. "But let's hurry. And you better help too, Freddie."

From the living room they heard a low earnest murmur — their mother's voice. And Papa's, sharper and louder. Adrianna listened. Mama was asking for money, telling him she couldn't get by on the allowance he gave her. Everything was expensive.

He liked good food and plenty on the table. But the holidays were coming — with gifts to buy for Saint Basil's Day, some presents for the girls here at home and others to send to the family in Greece.

When he answered, Adrianna heard a note of impatience in Papa's voice, and a feeling of dread came over her. She ran steaming hot water over the plates in the sink and wondered why Mama was spoiling this day by asking for money.

Now she heard arguing. Papa said, "There's plenty of food in the house. In the freezer. You have plenty of venison."

"Venison. That meat from the deer."

"Yeah, sure. I shot that buck last fall. And it still sits in the freezer. Why don't you use it?"

"That meat is tough. The taste is too strong. The girls, they don't like it."

He scoffed. "They don't like! It is you who don't like!" His words rasped through the house. "Look at you — how fat you are. And stuck in your Greek ways! Dressed all in black like my grandmother."

"My Greek ways . . . why they are wrong?" There was hurt in Mama's voice.

Frederika vanished, disappeared into their bedroom as always when Papa raised his voice, but Philomene continued to load the dishwasher as if she heard nothing.

"I keep my Greek ways." Mama kept the argument going; it wasn't like her. "Andonies . . ."

Papa interrupted. "Andonies! What is this — Andonies?" he demanded indignantly. "Here in America I am Anthony."

Mama's voice trembled, but she persisted. "Anthony, you know it . . . when you come back to Epirus — back from America. And you ask me to marry you . . ." She stopped and took a deep breath. "You give me promise."

"Ah-h, Ilone. Sure — I give promise." Was he mocking her? It seemed so to Adrianna. "And what about the promise you gave?

A promise of duty to your husband. You remember that?"

Alarmed and confused, Adrianna listened. She knew about her father's promises. Mama had often told her stories and anecdotes about the handsome young man, Andonies, who left his home in Greece and went to America when she, Ilone, was just a young girl. He came back some years later when she was seventeen, and his good looks and strong charm attracted her. She was pleased when he courted her, but she wondered how he would feel about remaining in Greece. She was the youngest of six children and her family's only girl, loved by her parents and brothers; she had no wish to leave them. She said this to Andonies, who now called himself Anthony, and he promised her then that they'd stay in Greece if she would marry him.

So they married, but five years later he changed his mind. He missed the opportunities he had seen in America. He had learned new skills there — construction and carpentry — and he was sure he could start a good business in California by using her dowry, still unspent, as his capital. Now the father of two small children, he felt he had no chance to earn a good living in Greece for his family.

After long arguments, he went back to America, and while she waited for his letters, Ilone knew she would follow. She couldn't remain in their village without him; her pride would not permit it. So when word came from him a year later that he was ready, she took their two small girls and embarked with great trepidation on a new life in America.

Listening to their quarrel now, Adrianna was certain that she could tell her mother's stories for her, she knew them so well. Many times Mama had told her about Papa's promises. But what was Papa saying about Mama's promises? What did he mean? Confused, Adrianna thought about her mother's work, all her duties. Surely she worked hard enough.

Mama stayed on her own train of thought. "When you take my dowry, you tell me we stay in Epirus."

"Ilone! I tried it. I could not. I had no chance to make good there."

"All right! So you go! And I wait. For a letter I should come. But again you give promise."

"What did I promise?"

"You say we will come back to Greece. Every year, we will come back. But it is seven years now — and we do not go back. I never see my family. Frederika, they do not even know her. They never see her." Mama stopped for breath.

Papa said nothing, and she started again. Her tone grew more desperate. "Your father and mother, they want to see you — their only son from America."

Papa was silent, and Mama waited. The silence between them filled Adrianna with dread. When at last Papa spoke, his voice was brusque. "My father and mother have other sons there. They have sons from their sons. I have not even one son to show them."

"Son . . . ? You got three beautiful girls."

"Beautiful! What is it, beautiful?" His mood was turning ugly. "Beauty passes. With no son, they will pity me. They will tell me that girls need dowries. But a son! All his life, a son is strength to his father."

Mama's voice faltered. "Andonies — you say it yourself. Here . . . in America . . . it is different."

"Yes. Different here. And here I stay."

"Anthony . . ."

"My business is good. I work hard. You have a good house — I built it for you. You have plenty to eat. No, I will not go back!"

"For a visit . . ."

"No! You only make trouble — with your crying to stay there."

Mama had no answer, and Adrianna remembered; although she was only six at the time of their visit to Greece, she still remembered the intense whispered debates between her parents—

Mama's entreaties that they remain there, giving up their life in America. She also recalled Papa's refusal.

For now, he had won today's argument; that was obvious. Mama would not get the money she wanted. And in the bargain, he blamed her for other things too — things that were wrong in their life together, things that Adrianna didn't understand.

✳

After their tasks in the kitchen were finished, Philomene returned to her room and shut the door. Alone with the gurgling and sloshing of the dishwasher, Adrianna dried her hands and smoothed Mama's linen tablecloth. She folded it, then walked down the hallway and hesitated before tapping lightly on Philomene's door.

"Who is it?" She heard a note of alarm in her sister's voice.

"It's me. Adrianna."

"Oh . . . Okay, come in."

Adrianna pushed the door open. It wasn't locked; no door in this house ever was. Inside, she saw Philomene sprawled on her bed, the blue and green bedspread rumpled beneath her, books and papers all around. Adrianna fumbled for words. "Phil . . ."

"Yes — ?" Philomene looked up from her books and smiled. Her eyes, dark and somber all day, took on a bright, almost lively expression.

"I want to ask you . . ."

"Yeah, what?"

"Well — it seemed like . . . I thought . . ." Adrianna took a deep breath and plunged on. "I thought I heard Papa in your room late at night — and I . . ."

"What — ?" Philomene's smile faded; her face colored.

"I mean . . . you know . . . like after you argued about the Halloween party."

"No, I don't know." Philomene's green eyes turned dark and

36

cold again; her voice became dull, expressionless.

Adrianna felt foolish. "Please don't be angry. It's just — I was wondering . . ."

Philomene said nothing.

"I heard him. And it seemed like he stayed a long time."

"In my room? You must have been dreaming."

"Oh . . ."

Adrianna no longer felt welcome in her sister's room. She left and closed the door behind her. It creaked. In the hallway, she stopped to look at some photographs on the wall, an array of family portraits. She studied a snapshot of a young couple taken in Greece years ago. She recognized her father. With his bushy mustache and unsmiling face, he still looked much the same. But the young woman who stood beside him, smiling and holding his hand — where had she gone? In the hard frozen silence between her parents this minute, Adrianna studied the photograph. The girl in the picture looked more like Philomene than Mama. The smiles were identical.

Chapter 6

"Our assignment today is a character study," Miss Delricco said at the beginning of Adrianna's third period English class. "A description of someone you know."

"How good should you know him?" Pete Lindstrom asked.

"Quite well. How else would you know what to write?"

Adrianna closed her eyes and pondered. She thought she might write about Sarah. But what could she say? Last year when Sarah left Middleton, she had promised to write every week and always remain best friends. But lately no letters had come, and after her own last letter — sent two months ago and still unanswered — Adrianna sadly acknowledged that Sarah probably had a new best friend in Denver. So how could she write about her?

She chewed on her pencil and wondered if she knew anyone else who was interesting. Silence. People thinking. Then pencils scratched, and she heard a small giggle from someone across the room. It sounded like Teresa.

"Can I write about my dog?" Pete asked.

"No — not really," Miss Delricco said, but then changed her mind. "Well . . . all right."

"Great!" Jenny said. "I'll write about my dog too."

Adrianna tapped her pencil on her desk, half-closed her eyes, and made up her mind; she would write about Philomene. Words formed in her head. As she scrawled them on paper, she lost track of time until startled, she heard Miss Delricco say, "Time's up for writing. Who'll read first?"

No one raised a hand.

"It's just a first draft. It doesn't have to be perfect."

Jenny raised her hand. "I will. I like what I wrote." The classroom was quiet, and everyone listened while she read. "Rusty, my dog, has feathery ears and a tail like a flag. When we go to the beach, I unsnap his leash and wade through the surf while he runs. Waves break at his feet, and he slurps at the foam. But when he tastes the brine, he shakes his head madly and comes galloping back to me."

"That's good," Tim Novak said. "It sounds just like him."

"Yeah . . ." Teresa agreed.

How nice for Jenny, Adrianna thought. Everyone liked what she wrote.

Jenny smiled. "Let's hear yours," she said to Teresa.

"No, mine's stupid. I tried to make it funny, but I don't think it is."

"Maybe it's better than you think," Miss Delricco said. "Let's hear it."

Teresa shook her head. "No . . . I can't."

Adrianna knew she couldn't either. Other people read theirs, but she didn't hear. Her eyes misted as she studied the words she had scribbled. "Philomene. Beautiful sister. Slim and graceful, everything I'm not. I want to be your friend, and I guess at your moods. Sometimes a smile lights your face, and your eyes sparkle. But other times, your eyes are like ice over still water. I see you near me, and I hold out my hand. But I can't reach you."

The words blurred, and the class went on around her. When the bell rang, she picked up her books and hurried off. She had a science assignment to complete during lunchtime; Mr. Mitchell had said he'd accept it even though it was late.

✳

In the cafeteria, Adrianna dropped her books on a table near the doorway and sat there alone. She reached for the brown paper bag in which Mama had packed her lunch — a sandwich of pita bread filled with small meatballs, an apple, some sugar cookies, and a thick slice of cake. She arranged the food on her napkin, but didn't eat. Instead she opened her science book and stared at the page of her overdue work.

"Hey, Ron! Look at that chow."

At the sound of that voice — dreaded, well-known to her — Adrianna looked up. Leland Baxter was almost upon her, and he had a friend with him. They came close, and Leland peered with gross gestures of amazement at her lunch. "What's that?" He pointed to her pita bread sandwich. "Looks like a coat pocket without the coat." He poked Ron and laughed at his own joke.

Adrianna didn't think it was funny, but Ron seemed to find it hilarious; they hung over her shoulder and laughed while she tried to ignore them.

"Hey, you guys! What are you up to?" Startled, Adrianna turned and saw Jenny. She was carrying a tray from the lunch counter.

"Nothing much. We're just having fun with Addie. Get a look at her lunch. No wonder she's such a blimp." Leland's tone changed when he spoke to Jenny; he sounded almost friendly.

"Some fun. Picking on other kids!" Jenny's voice rose, and people at tables nearby interrupted their own conversations to listen. Adrianna blushed. She wished she could disappear, melt down, just vanish from the scene.

Jenny ignored Adrianna's embarrassment. "Look at you, Leland Baxter! Skinny as a rail — with a face that's all covered with freckles. How would you feel if I insulted you, called you names? Like spotted scarecrow, for instance."

Leland looked abashed, and his face turned red under his freckles. But Ron protested. "How come you can't take a joke?" he asked, his tone injured. "We were just fooling."

Before Jenny could answer, Leland poked Ron and shrugged as if to excuse Jenny's missing sense of humor. Then together, they sauntered off.

"Well!" Jenny said. "The nerve of those guys."

41

"You didn't have to make such a fuss," Adrianna murmured. "I could've ignored them."

"Oh, no!" Jenny said hotly. She shook her head, and her mane of dark, almost black, hair flew around her face. Her amber eyes sparked with indignation. "You have to stand up to bullies. That's what my father says."

"Oh . . ." Adrianna said numbly and looked down at her unfinished paper.

"My dad told me . . ." Jenny rattled on, barely stopping for breath, "when he was my age, some kids picked on him. Pushed him around. Called him names."

"Why?" Adrianna asked, her attention shifting away from her own troubles.

"Well, he told me — he was just a kid, growing up in Chicago — and some guys in his school gave him a really hard time."

"How come?"

"He was small for his age. And wore glasses. And wasn't good at sports."

"So what did he do?"

A smile lit Jenny's face. "He took karate lessons. And then when they tried to shove him around, he sure surprised them. You better believe they left him alone after that."

"But . . . I don't see how . . ." Adrianna's voice trailed off. She thought about Jenny's father and how different her own problems were from his.

"Look — there's Teresa. And Tim." Jenny balanced her tray on one arm and waved with the other at a table across the room. "Let's go there."

"I can't. I have to finish this paper for Mr. Mitchell."

Jenny groaned. "That Mr. Mitchell — what a grouch! Well, okay — see you later." She flashed a smile at Adrianna, took firm hold of her tray and walked off.

Alone again, Adrianna found that her lunch no longer appealed to her. She stuffed her pita bread into the paper sack, added the cookies and cake, but kept out the apple. She tossed the sack into a trash can, then munched on her apple and concentrated on her paper. But she couldn't complete it, and when the fifth period bell rang, she collected her books and dragged herself to class. She sat at a desk near the back of the room and kept working. When the class ended, she handed her scrawled paper to Mr. Mitchell who looked up from the marks he was entering in his grade book and said, "Good, Adrianna. I'm glad you finished it."

She didn't answer; she had to hurry across campus to her sixth period class. Through the courtyard she went and along a wide path to the footbridge that spanned the creek. It was more like a park than a school here, with broad drifts of ivy carpeting the creek bank. She liked this part of campus and sometimes when the weather was nice, she ate her lunch here, sitting on a bench under a huge oak tree near the creek. Now as she rushed to avoid being late, she turned when she heard Jenny's voice.

"Hey, Addie! You don't mind if I call you Addie, do you?" Falling into step beside Adrianna, Jenny didn't wait for an answer. "We better step on it. That Miss Larsen — she gets really sarcastic if you're late."

Adrianna smiled.

"No dressing out in gym today. I hope I get to be partners with Tim."

Partners! Adrianna had forgotten about Monday afternoon folk dancing. Her heart sank; her smile faded.

Jenny giggled. "Oh, Addie — it's fun. You just have to learn the steps."

"I don't know . . ."

"I'll help you."

"Are you sure? Why would you bother?" Adrianna said uncertainly.

"I like helping people. That's how I am." Jenny was silent a moment and then said, "Maybe I get that way from my mom. Or my dad. They do things . . . a lot . . . for their friends." She grinned. "And sometimes, for people they hardly even know. My dad says my mom's an incurable altruist. Whatever that means."

"Oh . . ." Adrianna said, not at all sure that she wanted to learn folk dancing, even with Jenny's help.

They panted into the gym with the last stragglers and found Mr. Riley, the boys' gym teacher, shouting directions while Miss Larsen took roll. Adrianna straightened her sweater and fell into place beside Jenny. When Miss Larsen came to Adrianna's name, she looked up from her roster and said, "Adrianna Espirikos! How nice to have you with us today."

"Here," Adrianna mumbled. What a mouthful her name was, especially when someone like Miss Larsen called it out.

"Get into sets, everyone. This is the Virginia Reel." Mr. Riley's voice boomed up to the rafters and back.

Jenny prodded her. "Come on. I see Tim and Pete over there."

Adrianna froze for an instant. But when Jenny headed across the room, she gave her head a quick shake and followed.

At the record player, Miss Larsen started the music, and Mr. Riley yelled over it, "Okay, now! Six couples to a set. Does that work out?" Miss Larsen stopped the music while he counted couples. "Well, what do you know — five even sets. Ready now! Listen for the calls."

Miss Larsen started the music again, and Adrianna stole a glance at the boy facing her, Brad she thought his name was; she knew him just slightly. Looking bored, he turned and whispered to Pete who stood next to him. Adrianna could tell that Brad wanted to change places. No doubt he didn't want to be her partner, she thought, but she was sure that Pete didn't either.

She began to feel sick, her hands cold and clammy. But as the girls moved forward and back and bowed to their partners, Jenny smiled encouragingly at her. The sick feeling eased, and

Adrianna smiled back. She copied Jenny's steps and furtively wiped her palms on her skirt before taking Brad's hands to slide down the set. The music ended. The dance was over, and by some miracle she hadn't made too many mistakes; she had almost enjoyed it.

"Get ready for a schottische!" Mr. Riley called out, and Miss Larsen changed the record.

Loud groans and grumbling; everyone hated the step-hops and partner changes in this dance, but they followed Mr. Riley to a large circle painted red on the polished wood floor. Jenny, still partners with Tim, wandered to the far side of the circle, and Brad drifted away.

Pete stood facing Adrianna; he was her partner this time. He grinned at her, and she smiled back. But her smile faded when she caught sight of Leland, who was four couples ahead. Her stomach knotted and her feet faltered as she saw him stamping his feet and acting important. She stumbled through three repetitions of step-hops with three different boys before Mr. Riley called out again, "Partners change! Girls move up." That brought her to Leland.

"Well, here comes Addie the blimp!" he said in a loud, gravelly voice. He held out his crossed hands for hers. And dumb with rage and embarrassment, she took them.

Chapter 7

At noon the next day, Adrianna avoided the school cafeteria. With her bag lunch and a paperback book, she settled on the bench under her oak tree. Nearby, the creek rushed along. Fed by late autumn rains, it was swollen and filled with debris, but the ivy that covered its banks sparkled fresh, crisp, and green. The sun filtered its rays through bare branches and warmed her. She saw nobody near, no one to tease or bother her. It was quiet and peaceful here, far from the lunchroom's commotion.

She sighed with relief and took a bite of her sandwich, this one of white bread — filled with thin slices of meat and slathered with mayonnaise — a sandwich she had made herself. Yesterday, she said to her mother, "Don't give me pita bread anymore. No one at school eats stuff like that."

"So make it yourself!" her mother snapped back. And amazed at Mama's sharp answer, Adrianna did.

Enjoying her sandwich now, she reached into her lunch bag for the slice of sugar-frosted almond cake she had packed. Just then she heard a giggle; she recognized Jenny's voice and glanced up to see her talking and laughing with Tim and Pete as they strolled along the opposite bank of the creek.

Jenny saw her too. "Hey, Addie!" she called. "I wondered where you were!" With a quick toss of her head and an abrupt, "See you guys later," she raced over the footbridge and sat down beside Adrianna. "I have to talk to you."

Adrianna waited.

"I've been wanting to ask you to join our writing club. It meets after school every Thursday. In the library. I'm president."

"Oh."

Jenny smiled. "I mean — we're looking for new members. Kids who like to write stories and poems. Will you join?"

Adrianna took a small bite of her cake and deliberated. Finally, she said, "I don't know. I don't usually stay after school."

"I wish you would," Jenny urged. "We write things at home — and read them aloud at our meetings. And then everyone makes suggestions."

Adrianna didn't answer. She didn't know what to say.

"You'd like the kids. They're nice. Not like that stupid Leland. I think he's gross."

Shame and embarrassment swept over Adrianna as she recalled yesterday's lunchroom encounter. She wished Jenny hadn't mentioned it.

"Well — ?" Jenny said.

"Well . . ." Adrianna said cautiously, "I'd have to ask at home."

"You have to ask?" Jenny seemed surprised.

Adrianna was sorry she'd said that. "Well, yes . . ." she mumbled.

"But it's just an hour after school. Once a week."

Silence sat like a third person between them. Then Jenny looked at Adrianna's lunch and asked, "Are you going to eat all that cake?"

"Yes."

"You shouldn't."

"What's wrong with it?"

"Look at the frosting. It's loaded with calories."

Adrianna drew back, but Jenny didn't seem to notice. "Look at you, Addie — you've got really nice features. Take your eyes, for instance. They're so changeable. I can't tell if they're blue or brown. They're really pretty. And your skin. It's so clear. I wish I had your skin. You know, you'd look fantastic if you'd lose some weight." Jenny paused for breath before rattling on. "And quit wearing your hair pulled so tight in that ponytail. Let it hang loose. See—" She tossed her head back and sent a cloud of dark hair flying around her face. "Like mine."

Adrianna gasped. She felt unglued, taken apart. But Jenny — intent on listing Adrianna's good points and bad — just kept going. "Look at your sweater," she exclaimed. "It's totally the wrong color!" She picked at a loose woolen thread on the sleeve of Adrianna's tan cardigan sweater and let her hand rest there. "With your eyes, you should wear red — a really deep, strong red." She searched for the right word and found it. "Like burgundy — there, that's the color." But as she wound down her discourse, doubt crept into her voice. "Of course, you'd have to lose weight for it to look good on you."

Adrianna shook off Jenny's hand. And now Jenny noticed. "I didn't mean to hurt your feelings, Addie. I was only trying to tell you how pretty you could look." As Adrianna said nothing, Jenny's voice took on a note of exasperation. "You know, you're not the only one who has problems. Other people have problems too. Me, for instance." She brushed her long bangs away from her forehead. "See these pimples?"

Peering under the veil of dark hair, Adrianna saw a few blotches and bumps on Jenny's forehead. "Those — ? They're not much of a problem," she murmured.

"Oh, but they are! They're gross. I have to sit under a sun lamp to dry them up. And my mom makes me wear goggles, and they leave white stripes around my eyes." Jenny sighed.

Adrianna arose slowly and packed the remains of her lunch in its sack. Afraid of what she might say if she uttered a word, she clamped her mouth shut. But she couldn't remain silent. Her anger spilled out, and she blurted, "How come you're always acting so important and telling other people what to do? I wish you'd mind your own business and leave me alone!" About to stalk off, she paused and glared at Jenny. Then she sputtered, "And quit acting like those stupid pimples are such a problem."

With that she snatched up her purse, left her lunch sack and book on the bench, and fled. Jenny sat, her eyes wide, her mouth open.

*

Later at home, Adrianna sat at the kitchen table and stared at her books. The day had been ruined by her quarrel with Jenny, but now her anger was gone and she worried. How could she have yelled at Jenny like that when she wanted so much to be friends with her? She sighed.

Mama, stirring a pot of soup on the stove, looked at her and said, "Something bothers you?"

"No. Nothing."

"You look sick."

"No, I'm not sick."

"Mmn-hmn . . ."

"Well, my head hurts a little."

"Maybe you should lie down. Before supper. There is time." Mama dipped a ladle into the soup, then raised it to her lips, blew on it, and sipped. "Soup is ready," she said. "You want some?"

"I'm not hungry. I think I'll lie down for a while. Until my head stops hurting."

"Sure. Frederika is outside in the yard. I tell her, play quiet now." Mama glanced at the clock. "That Philomene — where is she?" She turned her gaze back to Adrianna. "You go. I put your books away."

Adrianna shoved her books aside and reached out to hug Mama. She didn't know why it was that when she felt sad and lonely, she needed to touch her mother and hug her. Now, Mama smiled. She patted Adrianna's cheek, and Adrianna felt comforted, but suddenly very tired, almost exhausted. She went to her room and threw herself down on her bed.

She half-closed her eyes, and the panda bear and dolls on Frederika's bed, the soft-colored pattern of rose-trellis wallpaper, the stark white of the ceiling all blurred. Still wearing her tan

50

woolen sweater and skirt, she lay still on her bed, but didn't sleep. She couldn't. She thought about wanting to be friends with Jenny. And then she decided. Tomorrow she'd tell Jenny she was sorry about losing her temper. And maybe, just maybe, she should follow Jenny's advice and try to lose weight.

But Mama might not like that. Somehow it seemed as if losing weight might make her seem untrue to Mama, might cause Mama to think Adrianna didn't like her cooking. And of course that wasn't true. Adrianna sighed. It was as if being plump like her mother was a comfortable and safe way to be. Safe? Safe from what? She turned away from that question. Not safe, certainly, from Leland.

Stirred by a craving for consolation, she reached for the candy in her drawer. The chocolates were gone, eaten late at night weeks ago. Some peanut brittle was hidden there now. But it was too crunchy for midnight snacking, and she regretted buying it. Her hand reached out and hung in mid-air for a moment before she pulled it back. No! She wouldn't eat any now.

The front door slammed, and she heard her mother ask, "Why so late?"

Philomene answered. "I was talking to some kids. We lost track of time."

"All right. Please, no noise now. Adrianna — her head hurts."

"Again?"

About to get up, ready to say she felt better and couldn't sleep anyway, Adrianna heard her father's step and his gruff hello. She pulled her blanket up to her chin and decided to nap until suppertime.

She slept hard and woke in the dark to the touch of a small hand on her arm. She heard Frederika say, "Addie — get up. Mama says you should come and eat."

She stirred. Feeling dazed and still tired, she tumbled out of bed, smoothed her hair back, and pulled her ponytail tight. She straightened her sweater and stumbled into the kitchen.

When the table was cleared after supper and the dishes washed, Philomene returned to her room, and Adrianna brought her books to the table. Mama studied her face. "Why you don't eat?"

"I don't know. I wasn't hungry."

"So?" Mama looked at her questioningly, but Adrianna had her own question to ask.

"Mama, can I join a club at school? A writing club?"

"Oh — ?"

"Is it okay?"

"With me — sure it's okay. But with Papa . . . You asked him already?"

"Not yet."

Mama gave a small nod toward the living room but said nothing more.

Adrianna hesitated, then left her books and approached her father. He sat in his easy chair with Frederika on his lap while they watched television together. Adrianna said, "Papa . . ."

He chuckled at a puppet show on the screen and didn't answer.

Adrianna took a deep breath and tried again, louder this time. "Papa . . ."

"Yes — ?" He turned his head slowly and looked at her.

"I want to ask your permission."

"For what?"

"For staying after school and joining a writing club, the one Mrs. Feldman told you about. It meets once a week on Thursdays." She said it all in one breath.

"You like that?" He stared at her quizzically.

"Yes, I do. And I've been pretty good, not coming home sick."

"Yes."

"Can I join the club?"

"Your mama said yes?"

"I already asked her. She said — if it's okay with you."

He smiled. "Okay, Adrianna. If you want. But after your meeting, you come straight home."

"Oh, yes! Thank you!" She threw her arms around him. He laughed and Frederika squirmed as she hugged them.

Chapter 8

Between classes the next morning, Adrianna found Jenny at her locker. She was hauling books out and throwing them in a heap on the corridor floor. Adrianna stepped over them and offered her apology. "I'm sorry I lost my temper at you."

Kneeling, Jenny pawed through her books. She tossed some of them back and said, "It's okay."

"Maybe I should try to lose weight," Adrianna said hesitantly.

"Here's that library book! What a relief! I thought I lost it." Jenny added it to her armload of books and struggled to her feet. "Maybe you should," she said to Adrianna. "But you're right — it's none of my business how much you eat. Sometimes I get carried away. My dad says I talk too much. I guess I did that yesterday." She slammed her locker door shut and grinned at Adrianna. "What a mess in there."

"You're not angry . . . ?"

"Me angry?" Jenny giggled. "No, you didn't hurt my feelings. Let's just forget it." She reached out and touched the sleeve of Adrianna's sweater. This time Adrianna didn't pull away, and they walked side by side down the hall to Miss Delricco's room. Almost there, Jenny stopped. "Hey! How about the writing club? You know there's a meeting after school today. Will you come?"

"Yes."

"Okay!" Jenny said. And they walked into class together.

※

The rest of the school day seemed endless. When classes were over at last, Adrianna shoved her books in her locker and hurried down the corridor. Jenny had promised to meet her at the library door. And there she was. "Hello . . ." Adrianna said, feeling suddenly shy. She played with a button that was loose on her sweater.

Jenny didn't seem to notice. "Let's go in. I told Miss Delricco you're joining."

In the library, Adrianna saw some students she knew and some she had never met. They sat in a circle of chairs pulled together, and Miss Delricco sat with them. "I'm glad you decided to join us, Adrianna," she said. "Come on over here." She pointed to a chair beside hers and then said to Jenny, "Let's get the meeting started."

"Okay. It looks like everyone's here, except Teresa. She told me this morning that she couldn't come." Jenny surveyed the circle of faces around her and said, "The meeting will come to order. The secretary will read the minutes of the last meeting."

Laura, the secretary, opened her notebook and read last week's minutes about their plans to publish a collection of writing. Adrianna listened and wondered about coming here; maybe joining this club wasn't such a good idea, after all. She leaned toward Miss Delricco and whispered, "What does she mean — publish?"

"We'll collect a poem or story from everyone. Then we'll put it all together in a book and make copies," Miss Delricco explained, but when she saw the expression of doubt on Adrianna's face, she added, "Well . . . but you don't have to."

"Oh . . . okay."

"Are there any committee reports?" Jenny asked.

Gary, a tall boy with glasses, said that his committee had studied ways to raise money for the club's publishing expenses, and they wanted to suggest a skating party. They had checked with the roller rink and even with a printer, Gary's uncle, who promised to do a rush job on printing the tickets so they could have their party before Christmas vacation. Everyone praised the suggestion while Gary sat back and smiled.

Before long, kids were reading aloud. They read poems and stories, things written at home and brought to the meeting. Gary read a poem he wrote about long-distance running, and Adrianna marveled at his self-assured manner, his easygoing way of taking suggestions.

The meeting went on to other business, and Chuck, another boy Adrianna had seen around school, reminded everyone to think about ways of organizing their book to include all kinds of writing. The meeting ended, and as Adrianna walked home alone, but not feeling lonely, she wondered if she could write something good enough for their collection.

*

"Hey, Addie! Wait up! Why didn't you wait for me?"

Adrianna stopped at the sound of Jenny's voice. "I thought you'd be riding your bike."

Jenny shook her head. "My brakes gave out yesterday. And my mom took my bike in for repair. On her way to school this morning."

"Your mom goes to school?"

Jenny laughed. "No. She teaches. Fourth grade at Emerson."

"Oh."

"My dad teaches too. Actually, he's a principal now, but he used to be a teacher. What does your dad do, Addie?"

"He has his own business. Construction." Adrianna didn't want to talk about Papa. Changing the subject, she said, "That was a good meeting."

"You liked it? Great! Will you write something for our book?"

"I don't know. I wouldn't know what to write."

"Sure you would. Remember when you wrote about your cat? You read that in class. It was good."

Adrianna remembered. "Well . . . maybe I could write about Greece," she said, although she still felt uncertain.

"Like what?"

57

"Like when I spent the summer there. At my grandfather's house."

"That sounds great. I wish I could go someplace like that. You're so lucky."

Adrianna was silent.

"Tell me about it."

"Oh ..." Adrianna said slowly, trying to fit words to her memories, "the sky is so bright there. And everything sparkles. The houses. The water. Even the mountain tops. But there's a cool shady place in my grandfather's courtyard. Under an old olive tree, with branches all gnarled ..." She stopped and searched for just the right words, then went on, ". . . like twisted arms reaching up. I loved to play under that tree. And sometimes I'd just sit there and look up through the leaves. It was like looking through green lace . . ." She broke off abruptly, embarrassed.

"Oh, Addie! That's almost a poem. Just the way you said it. Why don't you write it? And bring it to our next meeting?"

Adrianna wondered how she'd feel about reading such a poem aloud. Dubious, she nodded.

They walked on without talking until out of nowhere Jenny said, "Do you mind if I ask you a question?"

On guard, Adrianna said cautiously, "I don't know."

"Why do you always wear that tan sweater to school?"

Adrianna felt her face flush, but Jenny went on. "It's an okay sweater. I don't mean that it's not. It's just that it totally covers you. It looks like a sack."

Adrianna had no answer. At last she said lamely, "I like it." Wishing that Jenny would stop trying to change her, she summoned her courage and asked, "Do you like me for your friend?" She held her breath. What if Jenny said no?

Jenny's answer was quick. "Of course!"

Adrianna took heart. "Well then . . . could you like me the way I am?" She surprised herself when she said it.

Now Jenny blushed. "You're right. It's only . . ." Her voice trailed off into silence, and they walked on again without talking until Jenny said, "How about coming over and spending the weekend at my house?"

Adrianna was startled. "Oh! When?"

"This weekend, of course. The one coming up. You could come home with me tomorrow after school."

"I don't know . . ."

"Please come. I know my mom and dad would love to have you."

Adrianna wondered about the sudden invitation. Was Jenny trying to make amends for criticizing her tan sweater? Or did she really want to be friends? This time Adrianna didn't ask.

"Maybe if the weather's nice we could go to the beach. I'll ask my dad. He'll say yes, I'm pretty sure. And Rusty would love that." Jenny grinned. "He's my dog, you know." She stopped and squinted at the overcast sky. "Of course, it might rain this weekend. But then we could stay home and write. That'd be okay, wouldn't it?"

"I'd like that," Adrianna said, feeling pleased but confused as she trailed after Jenny's flight of ideas. "But I don't know if my father will let me."

"Ask him. And tell me tomorrow. Let's meet at my locker before the first bell."

They had come to the corner of Alta and Oak Streets. "See you tomorrow," Jenny said and went off to the right, up Alta, while Adrianna — wondering about how to get Papa's permission — continued on Oak.

Chapter 9

Waiting with Jenny at the curb of the school driveway, Adrianna scanned the line-up of cars inching toward them. "There she is!" Jenny cried. "In the Datsun, the dark red one behind the tan pickup." She waved wildly at her mother. When the car stopped at the curb, Jenny opened the door and propelled Adrianna into the back seat. "Hi, Mom," she said. "We better get going. There's no parking here, you know."

Mrs. Harris pulled away from the red zone and the students who clustered in groups, taking Friday afternoon leave of each other. Then she flashed a warm smile at them and said, "I'm glad you could come, Adrianna. Jenny's told me about you."

Wondering what Jenny might have said, Adrianna was struck by the likeness between Jenny and her mother. They were both slim and tall, with light eyes and dark hair, but Jenny's hair hung loose around her face, and her mother's was pulled smoothly back.

Jenny took over the conversation while her mother drove, and Adrianna half-listened as she savored the miracle of being here. To her astonishment, Papa had deferred to Mama's judgment yesterday, and she had said yes. So here Adrianna was, hugging a small suitcase, borrowed from Philomene with admonitions to take care and not scratch it. It held a toothbrush and pajamas, jeans and a blue turtleneck sweater that Mama had knit last year as a gift for her on Saint Basil's Day. While Jenny chattered on now, Adrianna thought back to yesterday when Philomene handed over the case and ransacked the hall closet for the pullover. Finding it, she had smoothed the blue cableknit wool and said, "Here, try this with your jeans."

Adrianna looked in the mirror and agonized. "Won't I look fat in it?"

"Sure," Philomene said, "but no fatter than in that tan sweater you wear all the time."

So this morning, Adrianna had packed the suitcase and carried it with her to school, where she forced it into her locker after cramming her books into Jenny's. And now here she sat, tongue-tied, holding it on her lap while Jenny rambled on about how the day had gone and what she'd done in school and about the writing club's plans for the roller party.

Pausing for breath, Jenny frowned, and a note of worry crept into her voice. Gary had called the roller rink and scheduled the party for a week before Christmas. But that was barely three weeks from now. And the tickets! She wondered if the printer would have them ready on time to sell to everyone at school. Maybe they shouldn't have planned for this party until after Christmas vacation.

"Don't worry, Jenny," her mother said. "If the printer promised to do a rush job, I'm sure he'll come through for you. And anyway, you only need a week for selling the tickets. Sometimes it's better that way. It keeps the enthusiasm up. Right now, let's make plans for this evening."

"Oh . . . okay," Jenny said. She seemed reassured.

"Your dad and I are going to a faculty party later tonight, and I'd like you to fix dinner when we get home so I can finish some school work. Is that all right with you, Adrianna?"

"I'd like that," Adrianna said, pleased to have a share in the conversation. She plucked at a tan woolen thread that had raveled from the sleeve of her sweater. She tucked the thread in and was glad she had worn her old cardigan; it was familiar and comfortable. She had packed the blue pullover but wasn't at all sure she would wear it.

"Our next stop is the grocery," Mrs. Harris said. "Let's get things that are quick and easy to fix. What would you like to eat?"

"How about steak and french fries?" Jenny said, but then shook her head. "No, not french fries. They're too fattening. Let's see — what can we have that's low-calorie?"

Adrianna caught her breath; there Jenny went again, harping on calories.

"Well, I think . . ." Mrs. Harris said, her tone matter-of-fact, "the steak would be good. And steamed broccoli. And a salad. How does that sound, Adrianna?"

"Okay, I guess." Slowly, almost smoothly, Adrianna let out her breath. To her own surprise, she didn't feel upset, after all, about the focus on calories.

"Will Dad like that?" Jenny asked.

"I think so," her mother said. "But anyway, we're going to that party after dinner. He'll get plenty to eat there if he's still hungry." She steered her car into the supermarket's parking lot and stopped in a space near the grocery entrance. She looked at her wristwatch and said, "Okay, let's see how fast we can be."

Dividing the items to buy, they raced through the store and made their selections. When they met at the check-out line in just fifteen minutes, Jenny giggled. "Some speed artists! That was pretty good, I'd say."

Her mother smiled and nodded in agreement.

They piled into the car and soon were at Jenny's house where Rusty's loud barking greeted them. Then in the kitchen, they chattered and giggled while they prepared dinner. When they served it, Mr. Harris said everything was perfect — the steak rare, broccoli crisp, salad tasty. Jenny beamed.

At the table, Mrs. Harris told about a fight in the schoolyard, and Adrianna stole a glance at Mr. Harris. She was curious about the boy — small for his age, picked on by bullies — that Jenny had told her about. But she saw not a sign of him now in Jenny's father. Not even glasses.

Interrupting her thoughts, Mr. Harris asked about Adrianna's classes. And he told funny stories about his day at school. But soon he became serious. He shook his head — his thatch of white hair a surprise to Adrianna over his ruddy skin and lively brown eyes — and complained that his school budget was cut again. Then out of nowhere, he turned to his wife and said, "Speaking of budgets, Beth, did you balance your checkbook this month?"

Mrs. Harris stared. "I'm not sure," she said. "Why?"

"The bank manager called me today. He said our account's overdrawn again."

"Overdrawn! I don't think so."

"I'm afraid it is. Did you keep track of your checks?"

She made a wry face.

Jenny's father ate without speaking until, breaking the silence, he said, "Honestly, Beth, I was embarrassed. I wish you'd be more careful. This is the third time — "

"I'm sorry. I guess I forget."

Mr. Harris shook his head again and uttered a small groan.

"Come on, Bob," Mrs. Harris protested. "It was just a mistake. You make mistakes too."

Jenny giggled and said to Adrianna, "My mom hates to keep track of money. And the bank keeps calling my dad. He says that's why his hair's turned all white. I think it's funny, don't you?"

Adrianna wasn't sure, but she nodded.

After dinner, Mrs. Harris folded her napkin. "Let's clean up. Then, Jenny, your dad and I are going to that party."

"Will you get home late?" Jenny asked.

"Probably," her father answered, his voice cheerful again. "But don't stay up past midnight. And turn off the television before you go to bed."

Jenny looked chagrined and said to Adrianna, "Last time I fell asleep with it on. It was still going when they got home."

"And Jenny," her mother said, "don't use the sun lamp while we're gone."

64

"Mom! I have to!"

"Not tonight. Tomorrow, when I'm home."

"Tomorrow we're going to the beach, I hope." Jenny turned to her father. "You still want to go, don't you?"

"If it's a nice day."

"Well, okay — I guess I'll catch some sun there." In good spirits again, Jenny cleared the table, and Adrianna helped her, delivering the dishes to Mr. Harris who loaded the dishwasher.

Jenny's mother smiled. "What a crew! I think I'll go upstairs and get ready now."

✳

Later, the girls watched television and ate popcorn, feeding great handfuls to Rusty. Then they slept through the night in Jenny's room where Adrianna woke the next morning to a drumbeat of rain. She squinted at the window and saw beads of water, clear as crystal, pelting the window and converging into trickles that patterned the glass. She glanced at the bed beside hers and saw Jenny, still asleep, curled under her blanket. Sounds came from the kitchen below — a muted clatter of dishes, a murmur of quiet conversation. The aroma of freshly brewed coffee drifted through the house.

Rusty stirred in his sleep and whimpered. The sound surprised Adrianna. Why would he cry like that?

Jenny bolted upright. She groped for Rusty's head and patted it, interrupting the whimpers and waking him. Then she rubbed her eyes and smiled at Adrianna. "He has these nightmares. I have to wake him or he starts to cry and shake all over."

"How come?"

"I asked the vet. He said dogs have dreams just like people. You know — well, I guess you don't — we got Rusty when he was a year old. From some people who were really mean to him. They gave him away when they moved back east — to New Jersey, I think. They said they didn't want a dog anymore."

65

"He's handsome — with all that red hair."

"Well, you should have seen him then. His hair was so tangled and matted we had to cut most of it off. But look at him now."

Rusty yawned and stretched, then lumbered over to Adrianna and thrust his wet nose in her hand.

"He wants you to scratch him," Jenny said. "But you don't have to. Just tell him to sit."

"It's okay. I don't mind." Adrianna scratched his head and the back of his neck, gently running her fingers down his feathery ears. He closed his eyes and rumbled a low, throaty sound, almost a purr.

"He loves that. He'd be happy if you did it all day. But tough luck, Rusty. We got to get going. Addie, you shower first. I'll straighten our beds."

Jenny flew through her tasks while Adrianna showered and dressed, this time in her blue pullover and jeans. Jenny grinned when she saw the sweater. "Hey, Addie — I like that color. It makes your eyes look all blue."

Adrianna smiled. She folded her tan cardigan into the suitcase, but her hand lingered on the soft wool and caressed it before she pulled the lid down.

✳

At breakfast, Mrs. Harris glanced up from the morning paper. "Looks like an all day rain. I guess we're housebound today."

"Oh, well," Jenny said, "we'll find something to do."

Her mother nodded. "You could help me in the kitchen, and then — "

Mr. Harris interrupted. "Bessie, please — no housework today."

"Bessie!" Jenny's mother protested.

Her husband winked at Jenny and grinned.

Jenny giggled and said to Adrianna, "My mom's name is Elizabeth, and mostly my dad calls her Beth. She likes that. But some-

66

times — when she starts running our lives too much — he calls her Bessie. She sure hates that name." Mrs. Harris shot a sharp glance at Jenny who lowered her voice and whispered to Adrianna, "And sometimes he calls her Bossy. I think that's gross, don't you?"

Embarrassed, Adrianna nodded. It seemed like a family joke. But was it? Did Jenny's mother think it was funny? Or did she feel hurt as Adrianna felt when Leland ridiculed her?

Mrs. Harris gave a quick laugh and said, "Well . . . let's put it this way. What would you like to do today?" As far as Adrianna could see, she wasn't greatly offended.

"I think," Jenny said, "first I'll sit under the sun lamp. Then I'll give Rusty's coat a good brushing. And after that — we already decided to do some writing."

"Sounds good to me," her father said. "I'll get a fire going."

Soon a fire blazed on the hearth in the living room. The girls sprawled on the carpet close to its warmth, and Rusty stretched out nearby, his red hair freshly brushed and shining. Adrianna chewed on her pencil while Jenny drew spirals on her paper and ran through suggestions of topics for writing. But nothing seemed right. At last Jenny said, "I've got it. Let's write about wishes. Wishes and dreams."

Adrianna drew a sharp breath. It seemed almost dangerous to write about that. Then thinking it over, she murmured, "Well . . . maybe." And she wrote. She wrote about the pleasure of being here and her wish that the weekend could go on forever. Tears came to her eyes as she wondered how she could ever ask Jenny to come home with her — for a weekend or even one night.

Jenny ignored Adrianna's tears. But her mother, who sat at a desk across the room, glanced up from her papers and asked, "Is something wrong?"

Feeling ashamed, Adrianna mumbled, "No, nothing . . ."

Mrs. Harris nodded and smiled. Her eyes still questioned Adrianna, but she picked up her pen and turned back to her papers.

Jenny reached for Adrianna's hand. "Come on. Let's go up to my room. There's a new album I want to play for you — with a great song about roller skating."

Adrianna took Jenny's hand, and with their papers still scattered on the floor, they bounded up the stairs together, Jenny giggling as she pulled Adrianna along.

Chapter 10

Adrianna rummaged through her locker after school while she worried about her overdue assignments. How could she get all of that work finished before Christmas vacation, now only two weeks away?

"Hey, Addie!" Jenny waved a packet of tickets in her face. "Here they are! These are yours."

Adrianna drew back. "My what . . . ?"

"Your tickets, of course. That printer! He sure took his time."

The tickets! Until this moment Adrianna had avoided all thought of selling them; she knew Papa would frown on it. And anyway, who would buy a ticket from her? She hesitated, then mumbled, "I can't . . ."

Jenny stopped short. "Can't—?"

"I can't sell them."

"But it's easy. This party'll be fun."

Adrianna nodded, but it didn't sound like much fun to her. She had visions of stumbling and falling all over the rink. "I don't know," she said doubtfully. "I guess I could try . . . But who could I sell to?"

Poised for flight, Jenny said, "Kids at school."

Adrianna shook her head; she couldn't picture doing that. But then an idea came to her. "Maybe . . . I could sell some to Philomene for her friends. Would that be okay?"

"Why not? They'd be like your guests — even though they're from high school. Here's ten tickets."

Adrianna held back.

"Come on, Addie! I have to catch some other kids too — before they all go home." Jenny tossed the tickets to Adrianna and sped down the corridor. Reluctantly, Adrianna slid them into her notebook, collected her books, and slammed her locker door shut.

✳

At home the driveway was empty, with no sign of Papa. But Philomene was there in the kitchen with Mama, rolling pastry dough on the counter while Mama worked at the table, kneading bread dough and punching it. Philomene dusted flour on her rolling pin and told Mama about a play her drama class was planning. She hoped for the feminine lead. "But if not that," she said, "for sure — I'll get the ingenue role." Struck by the sight of Philomene working with Mama and talking to her, Adrianna stood at the kitchen door and listened.

"Ingenue? What is this — ingenue?" Mama asked.

"That's when a girl acts really innocent and like she doesn't know very much. But she knows more than people think. And all kinds of things keep happening around her."

"Mmn-hmn."

"Mr. Murdoch, my drama teacher — he says I look just right for the part." Philomene brandished her rolling pin at Mama and imitated her teacher's Scottish accent, ". . . if you will brush your hair smooth — and smile — and open up your face."

Adrianna came into the kitchen. "And will you?" she asked.

"Will I?" Philomene returned to her rolling. "Yeah, sure I will. Hi, Adrianna."

Adrianna hesitated, then set down her notebook, pulled out the tickets Jenny had given her, and said, "I have to sell these."

Philomene drizzled honey and nuts on her thin sheet of dough. "What are they?"

"Tickets for a skating party. For my writing club. Want to come?"

"Why would I? Ask Freddie. She's in there watching television."

"You called me?" Frederika's head appeared in the doorway.

70

"No, Freddie," Adrianna said. "Please, Phil. I thought you could help me by selling some."

"When is it?" Philomene asked.

"Just before Christmas vacation. Friday evening."

"Friday — that's the last day of our tryouts. Mr. Murdoch wants to have the cast chosen by then. So we can study our parts during the vacation." Philomene paused, and Adrianna felt her stomach churn. Then Philomene said, "Well, I guess it could be fun for the cast. Like a celebration after the tryouts."

Mama looked up from her kneading and said quietly, "You asked your father?"

Philomene's face clouded. She looked down at her hands, shaping the dough into a long honey-streaked roll.

Adrianna persisted. "Is it okay, Mama? Can we go? Can we sell tickets to Philomene's friends?"

"Okay with me, sure. But with Papa . . . ?"

Philomene looked up, and her voice took on a sharp edge. "Will you skate, Adrianna? Or do you just want me to get rid of your tickets for you?"

"I don't know. It's been a long time since I skated. I don't think I know how anymore."

"That's something you never forget." Suddenly Philomene was helpful again. "We could practice. There's this place by the park. You know where I mean? They rent shoe skates."

Adrianna nodded.

"We could practice in the park, couldn't we?" Philomene said to Mama. She sounded enthusiastic now.

Mama looked from one girl to the other and said, "Ask him. Finish up here now, Philomene."

"Papa's home. I hear him," Frederika called from the living room and threw her arms around him when he walked into the house. "Hi, Papa. Did you bring me a coloring book?"

"Not today."

"But you promised!"

"Sure, I promised. But the time got late. Too late to stop at the store."

Adrianna studied his face; he looked tired, she thought, but in a good mood. "How did the job go?" she asked.

He seemed surprised at her interest. "Hard work today. But we did a good job." He turned to Mama. "What's for supper?"

Mama covered her bread dough and set it to rise. "Lentil soup and dolmathes," she said without smiling.

"Good," he said and took off his work shoes while Frederika ran for his slippers.

✳

After supper Mama dusted sugar on Philomene's fresh pastries and slid her loaves of bread into the oven to bake. Adrianna brought her books to the table; it was time to do homework. But her work lay neglected. She cast a quick glance at Philomene who looked back with a strange secret smile and then led the way into the living room. "Papa, Adrianna has to sell tickets for her school," she announced. "It's a skating party for her writing club."

"Has to — ?" Their father sat back, relaxed in his chair, his slippered feet on a stool, while Frederika flipped television channels.

"Ten tickets," Adrianna said hesitantly. "My friend asked me. Jenny. The one who's president of the club."

He nodded. "Who will you sell to?"

"I don't know. I thought . . . maybe . . . Philomene could sell some to her friends."

"Is this party like a dance?" Papa asked.

"No," Philomene said hastily. "Not like a dance. There are no partners. And no dance steps. Everyone skates alone. Oh, some people might hold hands. I could skate with Adrianna and hold her hand."

Papa gave Adrianna a long probing look. "You like to skate?"

"I don't know."

Philomene rushed in. "We could practice in the park — Adrianna and me. There's this place I know that rents shoe skates."

He listened, but said nothing.

"Please say yes," Philomene pleaded. "I could baby-sit and earn some money for our tickets — Adrianna's and mine. And the other tickets — I could sell them at school."

Unexpectedly, Papa reached out, and his fingers stroked Philomene's hair. "No need to baby-sit. Maybe this skating is good for Adrianna." With a smile that was suddenly expansive, he said, "I'll give you money for the tickets. No need to sell them, Philomene."

"But I want to."

"No," he said, his voice firm. "Adrianna, is this party for your school?"

She nodded.

"And you have to sell ten tickets?"

"Yes . . ."

"Okay. Sure. I'll buy the tickets. For a donation to the school. Philomene, it's no use to mix friends from high school with a party for Adrianna. But you can go — if you want — with your sister."

Chapter 11

Adrianna stood at the living room window and gazed out into the dark December evening as she waited for the red Datsun to arrive. Much earlier, before supper, she had changed into her blue cableknit pullover and a pleated skirt that she hoped would make her look slimmer, and now she stood drumming her fingertips on the sill while at this last minute Philomene dressed for the skating party.

After coming home late from school today, Philomene had whispered to Adrianna that she'd been chosen for the ingenue role. But while she bolted her supper, she told Papa she had stayed late in the library to finish her school work. And he seemed satisfied. He seemed satisfied, too, with the arrangements for tonight's party. Jenny's parents were driving and chaperoning.

When the Datsun pulled into their driveway, Adrianna called, "They're here! Come on, Philomene!" She dropped a quick kiss on Mama's cheek and started toward the front door.

Papa glanced up from his newspaper and said, "Have a good time. Be home by eleven."

In the car, they sat wedged on the back seat with Jenny who rattled on about how great the party would be and how much money they'd make; more, she was positive, than they'd need for their publishing expenses. She wondered if the writing club should offer some of that money to the scholarship fund.

Her mother, who sat up in front beside Jenny's father, turned and said, "Sounds good. But don't jump to conclusions. Better wait and see how it goes." Then she added, "You know, I feel nervous. It's been quite a while since I've skated. I'm not sure I still can."

"But you'll try," Mr. Harris said with a smile.

"Of course. You know me — always ready to try."

When they arrived at the roller rink parking lot, Adrianna saw a huge wreath perched high on a ledge over the building's main entrance; its bright lights blinked on and off, and it seemed to be welcoming them. But all at once she ached to run home. Her stomach churned, and she wondered what she was doing here.

Mrs. Harris looked at her face. "There's a small rink where you can practice. I'll go there with you. After that, we can come out to the main rink."

Grateful, Adrianna nodded, and they trooped through the double-doored entry, giving their tickets to a woman who handed them shoe skates from behind a long counter. The benches nearby were crowded with people who were trying on skates for just the right size. An organ, set in a niche, played a slow-moving waltz, and music poured into the hall, bouncing up to the rafters and back.

Mr. Harris inspected the girls. "Three lovely young women," he said, and added, "be sure your skates fit."

Adrianna wriggled her toes in the high-topped white shoes and gingerly rolled her legs back and forth. At that moment, Tim and Pete skated by; Jenny went after them.

Mrs. Harris took short rolling steps and extended her hand to Adrianna. "Let's go practice," she said.

Adrianna reached for her hand, but Philomene intervened. "Let's go this way. To the main rink. It's more fun there." To Mrs. Harris, she said, "We already practiced. In the park. Adrianna can skate. She just needs more confidence."

Mrs. Harris kept her hand out and started to insist, but her husband interrupted her. "Please, Bess . . ." he said quietly.

Mrs. Harris blushed and gave a quick laugh. "Okay, I'll see you later," she said and headed toward the small rink.

"Okay, Addie?" Philomene asked.

"I don't know." Adrianna's voice quavered. Her practice in the park was forgotten, and she felt totally clumsy. "Let me hold on to you, Phil. I think I should've gone with Mrs. Harris. My stomach is starting to hurt."

"No, it's not. You'll do just fine."

They took small careful steps to the polished wood floor while skaters streaked by on all sides. Filled with panic, Adrianna lurched to the wall and clutched at the railing there.

"You can't skate that way," Philomene protested. "Give me your hand."

Adrianna extended one hand to her sister, but held fast to the rail with the other.

"Let go of the railing!"

Adrianna took a deep breath and transferred her grip to Philomene.

"Okay. Now just relax. Don't look at your feet. And take long steps. Like you did in the park."

"I can't."

"Yes, you can. Loosen up. It's all right if you fall."

Fall! Adrianna pictured that disaster and shook her head. She tried to relax. And as she did, she found herself skating — maybe not gracefully, but moving at least in time to the music. She loosened her grip on her sister, and they traveled along side by side. Proud of herself, she wondered where Jenny was. Her eyes searched the crowd, but she didn't see Jenny. Instead, she saw Leland.

He saw her, too, and a smile lit his face as he changed his course and picked up speed. He zoomed through the crowd and before she could utter one word of warning to Philomene, he crashed into them. They wobbled and jerked; they swayed; they struggled to stay on their feet. Philomene steadied Adrianna and then turned to Leland. "Hey!" she yelled at him. "Watch out! You almost threw us."

Sailing smoothly beside them with a grin on his face, he offered not one word of apology before he streaked off, his copper hair aflame with reflections from the red and green lights festooning the wall.

Philomene seethed. "That stupid kid! I should trip him the next time around."

"No — please, Phil! Don't pay any attention to him." Her balance restored, Adrianna found she was skating, really skating, like everyone else, and she felt happiness expanding inside of her.

"Who is he?" Philomene asked.

"Just a kid who makes trouble. He's that way at school too. It's best to ignore him."

"Ignore! Sure — ignore," Philomene grumbled. But soon she stopped scowling and asked, "Can you skate on your own now?"

"I think so."

"Okay. I'm going to have some fun too. See you later." Philomene dropped Adrianna's hand and glided away, soon lost in the throng of skaters.

"Hi, Addie." It was Pete, smiling and offering his hand. She took it and adjusted her step to his in time with the music. They merged with the crowd.

She waved at Jenny and Tim who sped by, and at Jenny's parents, now skating together. Other people from the writing club — Laura and Gary, and even Miss Delricco — all smiled and waved at her. And as the evening went on, she caught glimpses of Philomene, alone and with partners, skimming by as if born with skates on her feet.

When the party was over, they returned to the car. Tired but delighted with herself and the party, Adrianna stole a quick glance at Philomene and saw that the vivacious expression was gone from her sister's face. In its place was a dreamy closed-over look. She touched Philomene's hand and whispered, "It was a good party. Thank you for helping me."

Chapter 12

It was Christmas Eve. Dusk was already falling when Papa brought a spruce tree into the backyard at home and propped it against the side of the house near the back door. Mama interrupted her preparation for supper and watched.

"Why you do this . . . ? she said.

"Do what?"

". . . bring home this tree."

"Why? For Christmas. To put presents under."

Mama shook her head slowly. "Not for us."

He didn't answer.

"Christmas is for church," she said. "To pray. Not for this tree."

Papa pruned a stray branch of evergreen needles and stepped back to study his work. Adrianna, who had come to the back door when Papa arrived home, watched him and reflected on past Christmas holidays when she was little. In those days, she and Philomene had asked for a tree so they could find presents under it and be like other children in the neighborhood. And their father had been willing.

But their mother was not. Christmas was for church, she told them; Saint Basil's Day, a week later, would be for gifts and gold coins. In this house — as in her father's, she insisted — there would be no tree cut down and brought home from the forest. And through all the years of Adrianna's childhood, Papa had followed her rule in this. Until today. Today, without one word beforehand, he was here with this tree.

Mama stood at the back door as if rooted there, but she said nothing more. Glare from the bright kitchen light cast her shadow into the yard, where Frederika — ignoring her mother's gloom — danced around Papa. Adrianna, standing in the yard in her mother's dark shadow, glanced back at the house. She caught sight of Philomene at the window, her silhouette motionless, framed in the bright square of kitchen light. But when Adrianna turned her eyes from her sister to Papa and then toward the window again, she saw that Philomene had disappeared, perhaps gone to her room to learn the lines for her play. She hadn't yet mentioned the play to Papa.

They sat through a supper of silence; Papa ate heartily but no one else did. Mama cleared the table after supper and loaded the dishwasher without asking for help; then she went to bed. Philomene, who also said nothing, returned to her room while Papa hauled the tree into the house and set it in a corner of the living room. It stood there, straight and tall, its forest-fresh fragrance wafting through the house.

Papa went to his car and brought back a large bulky package, which Frederika opened with cries of excitement, finding bright shiny ornaments, garlands of silver and red tinsel, and a gold-colored star. Together, they decorated the tree. When they finished, he fastened the star to the uppermost branch and stood back to admire their work. Smiling, he turned on the television and sat down in his armchair while Frederika edged herself under the tree's lower branches and played with her dolls.

When the clock in the kitchen said ten, Adrianna pulled the evergreen branches aside and said, "It's late, Freddie. Time for bed."

"Isn't it beautiful?" Frederika bubbled. "Aren't you glad Papa got it?"

"It's beautiful," Adrianna agreed. But glad? How could she be glad after seeing Mama's face? She held out her hand, and Frederika took it while Papa remained in his chair, half-dozing, half-watching television.

✳

The next morning, Frederika pulled her blanket up over her head and refused to stir. But Adrianna arose early with Mama and went to church. Back by mid-morning, they found Papa handing out presents. He held out a brightly wrapped box to Mama. "Here, this is for you. And a present for you, Adrianna. Merry Christmas."

Adrianna unwrapped the package he gave her and found a fleecy pink robe. Just what she needed, she thought, to make her look big and fat. But she said, "Thank you. It's so nice and fluffy." Kissing his cheek, she brushed her lips against his bristly mustache and wondered at the shiver its prickle sent through her.

Mama opened her gift and pulled out a shiny chrome-plated toaster. "Nice," she said. "Four slices of toast at a time."

In the kitchen, they ate a late breakfast; Adrianna gorged on thin buttermilk pancakes drowning in honey, but Philomene picked at her food. Papa touched her shoulder and stroked the angora sweater she was wearing, his present to her this morning. "I told the store clerk I want a sweater to look good with dark hair and green eyes," he said. "She told me this red is nice."

"It is. Thank you." Philomene hugged the feathery red angora. "I'm going to my room now."

"Why?" Papa asked.

"I have school work."

"On Christmas Day?"

"I have reading to do."

"What reading?" Papa played with his knife, scraping crumbs to the side of his plate.

Philomene ran her tongue over her lips. "I have a play that I'm studying," she said softly.

"So — ?"

"So my teacher, Mr. Murdoch, gave it to me. He wants me to learn some lines."

81

"Why?"

"For a part in it."

"Part? What part?"

"I told you — for this play he's putting on."

"A play on the stage?"

"Yes. He puts one on every year."

"You have to do that?"

"I want to. It's a privilege to get a part."

Papa pushed his chair back and stood up. "What else is there?"

Philomene rose too. "What do you mean?"

Adrianna watched with alarm as they eyed each other. They seemed to be playing a game, a deadly one, dueling for the one lightning stroke to decide who was winner. Still seated at the kitchen table, Adrianna glanced sideways at her mother, but Mama didn't look up from her plate.

"I mean," Papa said, "what else could you do — not to go on the stage?"

"Well . . . there's costumes and props."

"What is that — props?"

"That's all the stuff the actors need. Like furniture and such."

"This would be good."

"But I don't want it. I want to act."

Papa shook his head. "No, Philomene. Tell the teacher, you'll take this other job."

"No."

"It would be better."

"I won't. You can't make me."

"I can't make you?" Papa's voice was affable, his tone almost good-humored.

Color rose high in Philomene's cheeks. Still keeping her voice low, she bit off her words and threw them at him. "You're mean! I won't listen to you!" She shot a dark glance at him and stalked from the room.

82

Papa didn't seem bothered; he moved to the living room and replenished the fire before settling down in his chair to watch television. In the kitchen, Mama rubbed lemon and garlic on a chicken to bake, and Adrianna wondered what she was thinking. How could she act as if she heard nothing? Adrianna's eyes watered as she sliced onions for the stuffing.

Her mother broke the silence between them. "The onion, cut it under cold water. So the eyes should not water. And make it small pieces. Not big ones."

The day somehow passed, and when dinner was ready, Mama sent Frederika to Philomene's door. She stood, a small sprite of a messenger, and called softly, "Philomene, are you there?"

No answer.

Frederika persisted. "Mama says come to dinner."

At last an answer came. "Go away."

Frederika returned to her mother and said, "She won't listen to me." She eyed the food on the table. "Let's eat. I'm hungry."

Mama called, "Philomene —"

Silence.

Papa strode to her room and stood at her door. His voice boomed through the house. "It's time to eat! Christmas dinner is ready."

"Eat without me."

He shoved the door open and closed it behind him. In the kitchen, Adrianna saw her mother's face turn to stone. She felt her own stomach knot and her appetite slip away. Long minutes passed. At last Philomene and Papa emerged from her room, his hand firm under her elbow. "First we eat," he announced. "Then maybe we talk about this play." They sat down to dinner, but Philomene's eyes remained shadowed, and she sat at the table without eating or saying a word.

✳

That evening, Mama went to bed early again. Papa watched Christmas programs on television and Frederika, her head nodding, sat on his lap. Philomene secluded herself in her room while Adrianna sat on the couch and looked at a book Jenny had given her. It was a story about two teenagers who were caught in a murder mystery; she tried to unravel the mystery, but couldn't. Losing track of the clues, she leafed back through the pages and was startled when she looked up and saw Philomene beside Papa's chair.

"I want to talk to you," Philomene said softly.

"Later."

"Now."

"Sit down. Watch this show."

"You promised." Philomene kept her voice low.

"What did I promise?"

"You said if I came out for dinner, we'd talk about the play."

"I said maybe."

"How can you? You know why I came . . ."

Adrianna marveled at her sister's defiance and wondered why Papa didn't hit her as he had hit Adrianna other times, and for less. But he only said, "Be quiet now."

And then Philomene exploded. "I hate you!" she screamed. "You better not come near me again! Not ever!" She flew to her room, slammed the door shut, and kicked it. Soon her loud sobs rang through the house.

Adrianna winced. Frederika slid from Papa's lap and fled to the couch, to the shelter of Adrianna's arms. Their father did not seem disturbed. "Go to bed now," he said.

Adrianna took Frederika's hand, and they walked down the hallway together. She looked at their mother's closed door and wondered how anyone could sleep through the racket from Philomene's room.

Frederika whimpered. "Do I have to brush my teeth?"

"No. Never mind. Just get into your nightgown."

In their bedroom, Frederika buried her nose in her panda's ear and soon was asleep. Adrianna, envying her, turned on her radio and undressed; no brushing of teeth for her either. Lulled by the music, she dozed, until — stirred by a hazy awareness that not a cry, not a whimper, came from Philomene now — she sighed with relief, turned off her radio, and fell asleep.

Then through her sleep, she heard it again, the same husky whisper she had heard other times. It was Papa. She heard Philomene, her tone protesting, the words muffled. And Papa's response — his voice soothing, insistent, not angry. Soon all was quiet again.

Wide awake now, Adrianna wondered if she had dreamed or imagined the voices. She tried to fall back asleep. But she bolted upright and held her breath when she heard the squeak of a door opening, the click of it shutting, and the hushed tread of footsteps that went down the hall. The face of her clock radio shone green; the night was half gone.

Chapter 13

School was back in session, and the days swept on through January. Adrianna neglected her schoolwork and stayed away from her friends. Unable to concentrate, she found math problems too hard, history dates impossible to remember — and at lunchtime today she sat alone on her bench under the oak tree with a book of short stories, borrowed from the library. But the stories didn't interest her. She closed the book and stared at the creek, murky and sluggish now, a thin muddy stream with no rain since December. She reached for her lunch sack; in it were carrot sticks, wheat wafers, and a small carton of yogurt. She was dieting. It was her secret.

She had started the day after Christmas. At breakfast that morning, Papa had announced his change of mind, his decision that Philomene could be in her school play after all; he was giving permission. All through his explanation, Philomene sat without eating. She didn't smile. She didn't seem pleased or happy. Adrianna was puzzled. It was clear that she had won her way with Papa. Why then did she still seem unhappy?

Mama poured coffee and ate in silence while Frederika chattered on about her new toys. Adrianna took a thick slice of sesame egg bread and slathered it with butter and honey. She ate that slice and reached for another; she knew she was eating too much, but no one tried to stop her or even seemed to notice. Her thoughts turned to Jenny, and she wondered what Jenny might say if she could see her eating now. Picturing that reaction, Adrianna lost her appetite. She pushed her chair back and retreated to her room, where she lay on her bed and stared at the ceiling while she thought about Jenny and how popular she was at school.

Adrianna yearned to be popular, too, and she wondered if perhaps she would be if she were slim and pretty like Jenny. She lay still and wished for a magic wand to wave over her body and transform it into the slim graceful self she longed to be. But she had to admit that despite all of her yearning, there could be no magic here. So she made a decision. She would diet. At least she would try.

But it must be a secret. She would tell no one, not even Jenny; in that way, nobody would know if she failed. But if she succeeded! If she could maintain her will power and stay on a diet, then she wouldn't have to say a word to anyone. People would notice. Adrianna smiled at the thought of Jenny noticing.

Fired by resolve, she tore a blank sheet of paper from her notebook and searched in her drawer. She found a needle, still threaded, the one she'd used last Halloween to sew Frederika's bride costume. She jabbed at her finger and squeezed hard, shuddering at the bright drops that stained the paper. And beneath that red blot, she carefully printed her pledge to lose weight. She signed it in ink and searched for a safe hiding place. The drawer of her bedside table, of course.

Her drawer. In it was a fresh box of chocolates. How could she diet with it there? So that day after Christmas, she carried the box to the bathroom and flushed the candies away. After she emptied the box, she scrubbed her chocolate-smeared hands until she felt purged.

That was weeks ago, but her resolve remained strong and now back at school, she ate carrots and yogurt for lunch. Earlier today, Jenny had reminded her of a meeting in the cafeteria, a meeting with kids from the writing club. But Adrianna chose to sit here alone and eat spoonfuls of strawberry yogurt. She liked her secret; she felt good about it. But she didn't feel good about Philomene and Papa. She chewed on a carrot stick and worried about them. Chilled, she buttoned her tan sweater and opened her book. The words swam. She couldn't concentrate.

Puzzling about things at home, Adrianna stared at the creek, at the narrow trickle of mud bordered by banks of bright ivy. She lost track of time until she gave her head a quick shake and looked up again. She saw no one around and wondered if the bell had rung. Had afternoon classes begun? And then she saw Leland, crossing the footbridge that spanned the creek. Ron was with him.

Leland swaggered toward her and drawled, "Well, look who's here . . ." He grinned and loomed over her. How tall and thin he was! Freckles stood out on his face, and his hair glinted orange in the pale winter sun. "Let's see your book!" he demanded.

Adrianna tightened her grip on it. She turned away and tried to ignore him. That had worked other times; it would again. But it didn't. He reached down and snagged her book. Now she knew she would have to take notice of him. "Give it back," she said icily.

But he held the book high and teased. "You want it? Go for it!" He tossed it to Ron.

Adrianna searched the path with her eyes. Where was everyone? Where were the monitors who usually patrolled at lunchtime? She tried to keep her voice steady. "I said . . . give it back."

Leland hooted.

Ron snickered. "Here. I don't want your stupid book."

She reached, and her hand almost touched it. But with a quick twist, Ron pulled it away and lobbed it to Leland.

"Way to go, man!" Leland circled back toward the creek. His feet danced on the ivy, not even trampling it. Adrianna pursued him. He held the book over her head, and she reached again. But her hand closed on thin air, and her feet tangled in thick ropes of ivy. She tripped and tried to regain her balance, but couldn't and tumbled over the bank and into the creek. Leland and Ron stopped their game and gaped down at her, then dropped her book and ran.

Adrianna sprawled in the creek. Slimy mud, green with algae and mold, oozed over her legs and into her shoes. It matted her hair and smeared over her sweater and skirt. Out of nowhere a crowd gathered to watch as she clutched a thick vine that hung over the edge and pulled herself up. Now hands reached to help. "Adrianna! What happened?" It was Teresa.

Dazed, Adrianna stood for a moment, then wrenched herself free and fled, sloshing mud from her shoes as she made her way home. When she staggered into the house, Mama came from the kitchen and started to say, "What . . . ?"

But she cut her words short at the sight of Adrianna's face and propelled her into the bathroom where she peeled off the sweater and skirt and discarded them like rags on the floor. After pouring crystals of bubble bath into the tub, she turned on a rush of hot water and stood back with hands on her hips while froth rose from the crystals like magic. At last when Adrianna lay back in the bubbles and wept, Mama asked, "What is it? What happened to you?"

"Those boys!" Adrianna cried. "They're always teasing me! I try to ignore them . . ." She wanted to explain, but she couldn't; she didn't understand it herself. "I don't bother them. I don't even talk to them. I don't know why they hate me." Tears fell on the foam as her story spilled out.

Mama listened, her face grim. She trickled shampoo on Adrianna's hair and gently rubbed it in. Then she followed with cupfuls of water and washed the slimy mud out.

"Hi, Mama!" It was Frederika, home from her morning in kindergarten. "Where are you?"

Adrianna wanted to hide. "Please don't say anything," she whispered.

"All right," her mother said and went out. But when Papa came home, she told him about the boys who had hurt Adrianna.

"What do you mean — hurt?" he said.

"For months they tease her. Today at school they make her fall in the creek."

Papa glanced from Mama to Adrianna as he listened. Filled with shame, Adrianna hung her head. Her secret was out, and she felt somehow to blame, obviously unworthy of her father's love and concern.

✳

The next morning, Papa, with Mama beside him, drove Adrianna to school. They went to the office where Adrianna hesitantly, almost inaudibly, told her story to Mrs. Feldman. To her surprise, Mrs. Feldman already knew what had happened. Teresa had come to the office yesterday and reported Adrianna's accident. There had been a hasty investigation, and after some questioning, Leland and Ron had come forward and confessed their involvement.

In her office now, Mrs. Feldman said, "We're so sorry! This never should have happened."

"So!" Papa said sharply. "Why did it?"

"We were short of monitors yesterday. And there was no one out there at noon to . . ."

Papa interrupted her. "I want you to punish those boys! I should give them a licking myself." He pounded his fist on Mrs. Feldman's desk.

Mama nodded in agreement.

"You can't do that," Mrs. Feldman said. She seemed taken aback by Papa's vehemence. "But they are being punished. We want them to understand — "

Papa interrupted again. "How will you punish them?"

"Well, we've suspended them. And their parents are — "

"Suspended? For how long?"

"Well . . . I'm sure," Mrs. Feldman stammered, obviously flustered by Papa's interrogation.

"Yes — ?"

"For a month."

Papa nodded. But he wasn't satisfied. "And the parents — how will they punish them?" he demanded.

"Ron's parents have cut off his allowance. And they've restricted him to the house. Without television. And he'll have to make up all the schoolwork he's missing."

"And the other one? The one who makes all the trouble?"

"Leland . . ." Mrs. Feldman sighed. "That's a problem. His parents are separated, and his mother works. But she's talked to his father. And they've made arrangements."

"What arrangements?"

"The father will take Leland to live with him in San Francisco. For the month of suspension. It's hard for him. He may have to take time from his job. But he promised."

Adrianna cringed as she listened. Her hair hung loose over her face, covering her eyes, and through that veil she studied her father. She could see that he still wasn't satisfied.

Mrs. Feldman turned to Adrianna and asked, "How do you feel?"

"Stupid."

"Stupid? I don't understand. Why would you . . . ?"

". . . because they keep picking on me." Unbidden tears welled up in Adrianna's eyes and slid down her cheeks. "Why do they hate me?"

"I don't think they do."

"They must. They keep bothering me. What's wrong with me?" The hard question was out. She looked down at her hands, at the cuticle of her thumbnail and the raw, bleeding place she had picked there.

"It's not you, Adrianna," Mrs. Feldman said gently. "It's Leland."

Adrianna stared at Mrs. Feldman.

"He's the leader. The instigator. You know what that means?"

Adrianna nodded.

"He starts things, and Ron follows. They were looking for trouble yesterday. Any kind of trouble."

"Why do they pick on me?"

Mrs. Feldman was silent.

"Because I'm fat. Is that why?"

Mrs. Feldman shook her head. "That's just an excuse. It's not you that Leland hates. Not really. It's himself."

Puzzled, Adrianna pushed her hair back from her face and straightened her sweater, a brand-new green pullover; her tan sweater was gone, tossed out with yesterday's trash. "He's not in school today?" she asked tremulously.

"No. I told you — he's suspended."

"And you won't let him bother me when he comes back?"

"I promise."

"What if he does?"

Mrs. Feldman came away from her desk. She reached out and hugged Adrianna. "Trust me. I won't let him."

"Well," Adrianna said, "if you're sure . . ."

Papa stood up and patted the top of Adrianna's head. Mama planted a kiss on her cheek. Comforted, Adrianna watched them get into the white Cadillac, parked again in the red zone. After she saw them drive away, she fingered the pass Mrs. Feldman had given her and walked slowly, unwillingly, to class.

Chapter 14

Unsteady on her new bike, Adrianna kept pedaling and steering. A ten-speed like Jenny's, this bike was blue like her old one, but bigger and taller. Papa had given it to her last month, just a week after her troubles with Leland and Ron. He had wheeled it into the back yard and said, "Here's a new bike. For your birthday."

Puzzled, Adrianna replied, "But my birthday's in July. That's months from now."

"All right. So I'm giving it early." And he walked away before she could tell him how pleased she was.

Now as she rode beside Jenny, Adrianna said breathlessly, "I'll never get used to it."

Jenny laughed. "Sure you will. You told me you did okay on your old one."

"But these tires are so skinny. I can't keep my balance."

"Just keep on pedaling."

Adrianna tried to concentrate on her riding, but her thoughts turned back to her father and his way of handing out gifts after quarrels or arguments or embarrassments — as though he wanted to offer comfort, or perhaps even say he was sorry. How different from the way things were in Jenny's family, where they gave presents for happy occasions like birthdays. Only last week, Adrianna had shared in the celebration of Jenny's birthday, and now she remembered that wonderful time.

The invitation had come in a phone call from Jenny's mother. After talking to her, Papa had hung up the phone and said, "This birthday party for your friend, Jenny. Her mother invites you. Philomene too."

Philomene, who had come from her room when the telephone rang, exchanged glances with Adrianna and asked, "Where to?"

"San Francisco," Papa said. "For dinner in a Chinese restaurant. Next Saturday. You want to go?"

"Oh, yes!"

"And a concert. You know what kind of concert?"

"Yes, Papa," Adrianna said eagerly. "Jenny told me today. It's a concert at the Greek Theater in Berkeley."

"Greek Theater?" he said. "Very nice. Sure, all right. You can go."

And so when Saturday came, they accompanied Jenny and her parents to her birthday dinner. In the restaurant, they giggled as they tried using chopsticks to carry clumps of white rice from their bowls to their mouths. But as steaming hot platters of food kept arriving, they shifted to fingers and forks to work their way through the colors and textures and tastes of the feast. After dinner, they sipped strong tea from small cups, and Mrs. Harris gave Jenny a small box wrapped in bright paper. When Jenny unwrapped it, she found a black-banded gold wrist watch.

"Oh, it's so beautiful," she said softly.

Jenny's mother smiled. Her father patted her hand and said, "That's my girl."

Later, they went to the concert. Adrianna had never seen such a theater or so many people in tune with each other; she felt overwhelmed by just being there. The loud sound didn't seem to bother Jenny's parents who tapped their feet and clapped to the beat of the music. Jenny jumped up and down and screamed through some of the songs, but Philomene sat silent, entranced.

✳

Now as they rode their bikes home from school, Adrianna reflected on that day and said, "It was fun."

"What was?" Jenny asked.

"Your birthday party. It was nice of your parents to ask us."

Jenny smiled. Out of nowhere, she said, "Leland's back in school, you know."

"I know."

"Has he bothered you?"

"No . . ."

"What if he does?"

Adrianna didn't answer.

"Let's sit down and talk," Jenny said.

"I can't. I have to get home." Adrianna didn't want to talk about Leland.

"Addie!"

"Well . . . okay. But I can't stay long."

They found a grassy strip along Oak Street, parked their bikes, and sat down. "What if he bothers you again?" Jenny insisted. "What will you do?"

"Ignore him, I guess."

"But you tried that. It didn't work."

"Well . . ." Adrianna said slowly, "Mrs. Feldman said that if he picks on me again . . . ever . . . I should tell her."

"Okay. But I don't understand why you ever tried to ignore him. If someone's giving you a hard time, you have to stop him. Right from the start."

Adrianna was silent.

"It's what my mom says. My dad too. You have to tell whoever it is to get off your back. Take a hike. Get lost."

Adrianna half-smiled. She couldn't imagine herself saying things like that to Leland. But soon her smile faded, and she said, "I just wanted to hide. Or shrivel up when he called me names. I know I'm too fat."

"Yeah. But he has no right . . ." Jenny's voice trailed off. She stared for a moment at Adrianna, then said, "You know, you look thinner to me lately."

The moment was sweet. All at once Adrianna forgot about her troubles with Leland; she beamed.

"You've lost weight?"

Adrianna nodded.

"How much?"

"Fourteen pounds."

"Fantastic!" Jenny threw her arms around Adrianna and hugged her. Laughing, they sprawled on the grass; giggling, they sat up again.

Adrianna arose and held out her arms like a fashion model. She turned around slowly to show off her new outfit, a tailored blouse and matching skirt.

"Yeah! You are thinner. You sure are!" Jenny exclaimed. "And I like that color on you. The dark red makes your eyes look all blue and sparkling."

"I've been losing almost three pounds a week," Adrianna said, feeling suddenly shy and unsure about telling her secret. But she went on. "And I exercise every day. Mama keeps Freddie out of our room while I do calisthenics."

"Great! And we can go bike riding on the road by the creek. That'll take off a few pounds."

"Okay. But I have to go now. What time is it?"

Jenny consulted her new watch. "Almost four."

"I'm late! I promised to be home early. I have to baby-sit."

"Baby-sit? How come?"

Ready to start off, Adrianna paused and said, "Some afternoons I watch Freddie. To help my mother."

"Oh . . . ?"

Adrianna was careful to say nothing more. She was, in fact, keeping it secret that Mama had started a business of cooking and baking for other people. It all began after Christmas when some ladies at church had asked for her recipes, and then some asked her to prepare special dishes for their parties and other affairs. She did this in the mornings at home now and made her deliveries by taxi when Adrianna came home from school. Proud of her work and the money she earned, Mama was pleased. "Is good business, this catering," she said to Adrianna. Things were going so well that she hoped to give cooking lessons at church, in the kitchen just off the main meeting hall. So Adrianna helped her to keep it all secret from Papa by watching Frederika while Mama worked.

Now while Adrianna straddled her bike, Jenny said, "Not on Thursdays, I hope. You don't want to miss our club meetings — "

"No, not on Thursdays." Relieved that Jenny asked nothing more, Adrianna balanced herself on her bike and shoved off.

She heard Jenny shout after her, "Faster! Keep your wheel straight and go faster!" She straightened her shoulders and pumped her legs harder. Her bike straightened, too, and she rode smoothly all the way home.

※

At home, the kitchen was empty. Adrianna looked through the window and saw Frederika playing in the shade of an almond tree that grew in their back yard. She opened the back door and called, "Did Mama leave?"

"Yep."

"Was she carrying something?"

"Uh-huh. A big pan. It was all covered up."

"Who's here with you?"

"Philomene. In her room."

Adrianna dropped her books on the table, walked down the hallway, and knocked at Philomene's door. There was no answer. She pushed the door open and poked her head in. Seated at her desk, Philomene looked up from her books and said coldly, "Where were you? Mama said you would baby-sit."

"I'm sorry. I was talking to Jenny. The time got away from me."

"You're lucky I came home early." Philomene looked down at

99

her books as if ending the conversation. But Adrianna ventured in and sat on her sister's bed. Once there, she wondered what to say. She looked down at the flowered spread, rumpled beneath her, and said hesitantly, "I'm losing weight. Have you noticed?"

"Really? How much?"

"Fourteen pounds so far. I'm going to lose more. Mama's helping me."

"How?" Philomene sounded amused.

"She's making less fried foods. More broiled."

"She is?" Philomene hadn't noticed.

"Yes. And most days, I take yogurt for lunch."

This Philomene had noticed, having taken Adrianna's lunch sack by mistake one day last week. She laughed, and the ice between them was broken. She pushed her books aside and came to sit beside Adrianna. "I'm glad you don't mind eating that stuff," she said. "I hate it. But Addie, your face is so pretty . . . If you ever get thin enough to have a nice figure . . ." She stopped, and they looked at each other.

Adrianna felt suddenly chilled by the unspoken words that hung heavy between them. Then she gathered her courage and asked, "Phil, what's bothering you?"

"Bothering me . . . ? Why? What could be bothering me?" Philomene avoided Adrianna's eyes.

"You keep to yourself so much. It's like you have a secret."

"A secret? Me? You're imagining things. I'm just busy. It's hard to learn all my lines."

"But sometimes I get a feeling. It's like you're in trouble."

Philomene smiled, but her green eyes remained shaded and somber. "I like your hair, long and loose like this."

"Don't change the subject. Can't you tell me what's wrong? Maybe I could help you."

"I already told you. There's nothing wrong."

Adrianna wanted to ask Philomene about the sounds in her room late at night, but she remembered the chill in her sister's eyes when she mentioned those sounds before, months ago. So instead she reached for Philomene's hands and said softly, "I hate when you get so . . . I don't know . . . so cold. It's like you go far away from me."

Philomene wrapped her arms around Adrianna, and they sat a long time, silently holding each other. Then she pulled away. "Dear Addie," she whispered, "there's no way you can help me. But thanks for asking."

Chapter 15

"Look at me!" Frederika called from the almond tree in their backyard. In bloom early this year, the tree was covered with radiant pink blossoms, and high on a branch, her face framed by flowers, Frederika called down to Adrianna.

Seated in the shade of a willow tree halfway across the yard, Adrianna closed the book she was reading and looked up in alarm. "What are you doing up there?" she asked.

"Making a flower nest."

"No, Freddie! Come down."

"I like it here."

Adrianna dropped her book and hurried to stand under her sister's tree. "Climb down," she said sternly. "Now! Right this minute!"

"No. I need some more flowers." Frederika collected more blossoms and arranged them around her.

"Freddie! Be careful!"

But Frederika ignored her sister. Still on her perch, she stretched to a cluster of blooms overhead. The branch swayed.

Adrianna held her breath.

"I need more . . ." Frederika reached higher and, still reaching, lost her balance and tumbled through branches and blossoms until she lay sprawled on the ground.

Adrianna rushed to her side. "Are you all right?"

"I don't know . . ." Frederika's voice quavered with surprise and indignation. "My leg . . . it feels funny."

Adrianna inspected her sister's legs. The left leg hung strangely awry in her blue jeans, as if attached loosely like a rag doll's to the rest of Frederika's body. She took a deep breath and tried to keep her voice steady. "I think your leg is broken. Don't move. I'll call Mama."

She ran to the house and telephoned the church meeting hall where she knew Mama was giving a lesson. When her mother answered the phone, Adrianna said urgently, "Come home quick! Freddie's hurt!" Then she snatched up a blanket and raced back to her sister who lay crumpled beneath the almond tree, the radiant pink blooms she had plucked for her nest now crushed and scattered around her.

Adrianna spread the blanket over Frederika and gently mopped at her tears. "You'll be okay, Freddie," she murmured. "Mama's on her way home."

Soon a taxi drove up, and their mother jumped out. She gathered Frederika up in her arms and carried her to the back seat, cradling her there, while the driver — with Adrianna beside him — sped to the hospital.

※

That evening, Frederika, her leg in a cast, lay on the couch in the living room and complained, "This cast is too heavy!" Between sobs she swallowed spoonfuls of chicken soup that Mama fed her.

Papa sat at the table in the kitchen and glowered. Philomene glanced at him and said, "Come on, Addie. Let's get supper out." She moved to the stove where a roast, long done, remained warm in the oven.

"I'm sorry . . ." Adrianna said hesitantly as she set the table.

"Sorry!" Papa's voice was gruff. "What good is it, sorry? How come you let Frederika climb up there?"

"I didn't see. I was reading."

"Reading! All the time reading!" His voice rose. "Now her leg is broken."

"Don't get excited," Philomene said, her voice soft and soothing. "It was an accident."

"You!" he said sharply. "Where were you when Frederika was hurt?"

"At school. Practicing. You said I could."

"Practicing!" He seethed. His anger seemed to feed on itself, and he shouted, "Ilone!"

Mama stood in the doorway with Frederika's empty bowl in her hand. Turning, he saw her and lowered his voice. "So! Where were you today?"

"In church."

"In church? How come on a weekday in church?"

"I give lesson there."

He stared. "What lesson?"

"Cooking lesson. The ladies from church, they want I should teach them special dishes. They pay me."

Papa's face flushed, but Mama went on. "What else should I do? I tell you I need money. For house. For girls. For presents to send home to Greece. But you say no. So what should I do? I give lessons for money."

"No!" Papa roared at her.

They heard Frederika whimpering in the living room, but no one answered her cry.

Mama stood her ground. "I do my work here. For you. Now I do other work too. For me."

Adrianna was filled with dismay. "Please, Papa . . ." she pleaded, "don't yell at Mama. It's not her fault. I . . ."

"Fault!" He wheeled on Adrianna, his face suddenly livid. "You tell me — whose fault!" He pulled his arm back and hesitated, then drove his fist forward in a smooth powerful motion and hit the side of her head. Her head jerked; her ears rang; tears flooded her eyes.

He seemed driven by a fury beyond his control as he struck her again. And again. She cowered and hunched herself over. Throwing her arms up over her head, she protected her face and tried to ward off his blows. He grabbed her shoulders and shook her. Her head bobbed; her teeth rattled. She went limp, and a kaleidoscope, broken bits of memories, flashed through her head and became one with this moment. "Don't, Papa!" she cried. "Don't hit me again! I'm sorry."

"Stop it!" Philomene screamed while Mama grabbed his arms. Together, they pulled him away — and Adrianna slumped, sobbing, to the kitchen floor.

"No more!" Mama cried. "No more you hit her!" Kneeling, she cradled Adrianna and stroked her head, murmuring over and over, "No more, Adrianna, no more . . ."

Flushed and disheveled, Philomene glared at Papa. And for a moment, he stared back. Then his eyes fell, and he muttered, "Women! What a houseful of women!" He turned his back on them and stormed from the room. The front door slammed; its vibrations rattled the windows and shook through the house.

Then quiet descended, and through that stillness they heard Frederika's voice, shrill with fright, calling them.

"Go to her, Philomene," Mama said.

"Take it easy, Freddie! I'm coming!" And Philomene ran to her sister.

Adrianna lay on the floor. "Oh, Mama . . ." she cried and buried her face in her mother's lap. She didn't know how long she lay there while Mama stroked her head and whispered words of comfort. Then through the blur of her misery and pain, she felt Mama's strong hands pulling and lifting her up. She struggled to her feet and stumbled to bed where she covered her head with her blanket and flooded her pillow with tears. Her mother sat with her — until at last, soothed by Mama's touch, lulled by her voice, Adrianna dropped off to sleep.

✳

She woke in the night to find her mother gone. In the bed next to hers, Frederika slept, her leg in its cast resting high on a pillow. But someone was near, reaching out to her.

"Adrianna . . ."

"Papa . . . ?"

"Sorry."

Did she hear a catch in his voice? Confused, she said nothing.

"Sorry — I hit you too hard."

Why? Papa, why is it me that you hit all the time? The words cried out in her head, but she didn't say them aloud. She thought she had no tears left, but they slid down her face to her pillow again.

"I forgot my temper . . ." His voice was gentle; his hand smoothed her hair. But then his voice hardened. "Attention, Adrianna. You have to pay better attention."

"Oh, Papa . . ."

"You dream all the time, your face in a book. You have to pay more attention when you take care of your sister."

Adrianna accepted his blame. "I'm sorry," she whispered. "I didn't mean to hurt her. I'll try to do better."

"All right." His voice, warm and loving again, told her his anger was gone. She had been inattentive and careless, deserving of punishment, but he had been wrong to hit her so hard. And then through the blanket that covered her, she felt his hand lightly and smoothly caressing her leg.

Her stomach turned. Bitter bile rose up in her throat, and she threw back her blanket and jumped out of bed. "Sorry!" she gasped and fled to the bathroom. There, rocked by nausea, she stood over the sink and threw up — until gradually she quieted her stomach and took back control of her breathing.

When she made her way back down the hallway, he was gone, nowhere to be seen. The door to the bedroom he shared with Mama was closed. Was he there? She shut her own door behind her and wished for a lock on it. In the dark, Frederika sighed but slept on.

✳

It was near morning when Adrianna fell asleep and almost noon when she awoke. Bruised and aching, she stumbled into the kitchen and found Mama there. Television noises blared from the living room where Frederika, propped up by pillows, lay on the couch.

Mama, her eyes clouded, looked at Adrianna and said, "You want I should fix you some lunch?"

Adrianna nodded, but when Mama brought her a salad and toast, she couldn't eat. The toast tasted like sawdust, the salad like grass. She returned to her bed and spent the day there, sleeping and reading, trying to erase last night's disaster from her thoughts.

That afternoon, Papa came home early. "Adrianna — " he called.

She didn't answer. She heard him ask, "Where is she?"

"Sleeping," Mama said curtly.

He called again. "Adrianna! I have a present for you."

She pulled on the pink fleecy robe he had given her last Christmas and came from her room. Wary, she stood poised for flight.

"I have something for you. In my car." He left and soon returned with a rough-textured black case. "Here is a typewriter. For your schoolwork." He handed it to her and cautioned, "It's heavy. Be careful."

She set it on the table and turned the small shiny key in its lock, then lifted the cover and found a brand-new portable electric typewriter. "But I don't know how to type," she said.

"You could learn. I see you always writing. It will be better with a typewriter."

She roused herself and kissed his cheek. Trying to ignore the tremor that went through her, she said, "Thank you, Papa."

Chapter 16

"Addie! Stop dreaming!"

"What . . . ?" Adrianna shook her head, and the papers on the library table came back into focus. She glanced around and saw everyone else hard at work, drafting the pages for their book.

"I'm talking to you," Jenny said impatiently. "I need your opinion."

"I didn't hear you."

"Well! Look at this. What do you think of the layout?"

Adrianna narrowed her eyes and studied Jenny's handprinted page. "That's nice. The spacing is good."

"Yeah. I think so too." Jenny sighed. "I'm tired. My back feels like it's broken." She glanced at her wrist watch and compared it to the clock on the library wall. "Four o'clock. We better quit."

Adrianna felt her heart sink. She knew her mother wanted her home early today. "I have to get home! I'm late."

"Me too," Jenny said, and called out to Miss Delricco who was working at another table with Gary. "Shouldn't we stop now?"

"Right!" Miss Delricco said. "Listen up, everyone. Stack everything on the shelves in this cupboard. Then gather around. I want to talk with you and make some plans."

They cleared the library tables and, with loud sighs and groans, stored their unfinished pages in the cupboard. "Who can stay late next Thursday to finish the layouts?" Miss Delricco asked. "You're doing a fine job. But we're running out of time — with spring vacation coming up so soon."

"I'll stay."

"I will too." Voices rang out. But Adrianna didn't join them.

"Good," Miss Delricco said. "That wraps it up for today."

With gratified murmurs and comments, they stood — in pairs and in groups — and chatted before they gathered their sweaters and backpacks and drifted out of the room. Hurrying off by herself, Adrianna paused when she heard Jenny call, "Hey, Addie! Wait up!"

"I'm walking. I didn't ride my bike today."

"Neither did I." Jenny fell into step beside her, and they left the school campus together.

As they walked down Oak Street, Adrianna felt Jenny's eyes on her blue sweater, the one Mama had knit. She had worn it for days, its long sleeves and high turtleneck hiding her bruises, the marks left by Papa's beating.

"Isn't that sweater too warm now?" Jenny asked. "It's such a hot day."

"What . . . ? This? Oh, no . . . it's okay."

"Well!" Jenny said. "Too warm for me. It's like summer today. Hardly like April!"

"Mmn-hmn."

They lapsed into silence and were almost at Alta and Oak when Jenny said hesitantly, "Addie . . . have I done anything to hurt your feelings? If I did, I'm sorry. I didn't mean to. I know I talk too much. And sometimes I say things I don't mean."

Startled, Adrianna looked up from the cracks she was counting in the sidewalk. "Oh, Jenny . . . no . . ."

"You've been so quiet lately. For days." Jenny paused as if searching for words. "Like distant . . . aloof."

Adrianna's eyes misted. She wanted to tell Jenny that their friendship was the only good part of her life. But how could she say that?

They walked on without talking until Jenny said, "We're going to the beach, Sunday. My mom and dad and me. And Rusty. Will you come?"

"Oh . . . I don't know." Adrianna thought about the bruises on her arms and back. She was sure she would die of shame if

Jenny saw them.

"Addie . . ."

"Mmn-hmn."

"Are you listening?"

"Yes."

"Do you have to ask permission?"

"For what?"

"For going to the beach, of course."

"I guess so."

"Okay. Then ask. And tell me tomorrow." And with a quick wave of her hand, Jenny turned off at Alta Street.

Alone with her doubts and misgivings, Adrianna continued on Oak. By the time she reached home, she had made up her mind. She would ask for permission. She was sure Papa would say no, and that would settle it. Tomorrow, she would tell Jenny that she couldn't go.

She approached him after supper. He listened to her and then said, "All right, Adrianna. You can go. But be careful by the water."

Amazed that he wanted to please her, she decided to go. She would wear her turtleneck sweater again and hide the bruises, now turning purple and brown, on her shoulders and arms. She gave brief, silent thanks that she had protected her face through his beating; not a bruise or mark visible there.

❋

When the Datsun pulled up Sunday morning, Adrianna hurried out of the house and into the car to sit on the back seat with Jenny and Rusty. Then off they went to the ocean. As they threaded their way through the last ridge of coastal hills, she saw that the day — warm and sunny at home — was cold and overcast here.

They parked on a bluff overlooking the beach and scrambled out of the car. Jenny complained. "Look at that sky! I thought

I'd get some sun on my face. I need it. But it sure doesn't look like it now."

"Don't jump to conclusions," her mother said. "The sun may come out yet. Let's unload the car."

Jenny unsnapped Rusty's leash and reached for his ball. "Oh, well," she said, "at least we'll give Rusty a workout."

Carrying their gear, they trudged single file through the dunes. Mr. Harris led the way while Rusty charged ahead. Adrianna — reassured by the cold dripping fog — adjusted her pullover sweater, hanging loose over her jeans, and followed close behind Jenny. She carried a backpack; in it were shorts, packed at Jenny's insistence. But who would want to wear shorts here in this weather?

They tramped through tall grasses and straggles of ice plant until Mrs. Harris spotted a sandy ridge, held fast by saltbush. "Good shelter here," she said. "Let's take it." They halted their march, tossed their blanket and other gear down, then kicked off their shoes and scuffed on bare feet to the shore. The beach was deserted.

Mr. Harris reached for his camera. "I'd like to get some shots through the mist. The fog may burn off soon. And things will look different then. Much more ordinary." He surveyed the beach. "Not a soul here but us. Guess I'll walk down by the shore for awhile."

"Wait for me," his wife said and turned to the girls. "Want to come?"

Jenny shook her head. "No — we'll stay here and let Rusty retrieve. If that's okay with you, Addie."

Adrianna nodded, although she would have liked to walk along the beach with Jenny's parents.

Mrs. Harris looked at the waves and said, "Stay out of the water."

"Oh, Mom!"

But Jenny's father said firmly, "The surf is too heavy today.

Let Rusty run on the shore."

Adrianna dug her bare toes in the sand and tested the foam that swirled up in her prints. It was cold. Her eyes followed Jenny's parents until they were far down the beach, where they stopped to examine ropes of seaweed and contortions of driftwood. She watched them snap pictures and wander on.

Jenny turned her back to the ocean and lobbed Rusty's ball toward the dunes. It flew high in an arc overhead, and Rusty ran for it. Skidding to a stop where it fell, he clamped his jaws around it and, without even panting, trotted back to Jenny and dropped the red ball at her feet.

She wiped it on her sweat shirt and patted his head. "That's not much exercise, is it?" She stopped and pointed up at the sky, just beginning to lighten now. "Look, Addie, the fog is starting to lift. The sun might come out, after all."

Rusty barked.

"Okay! Now get this!" Jenny pulled her arm back and hurled the ball straight down the beach. It flew fast. Skimming low, it landed on a water-washed strand and rolled toward the ocean.

Rusty raced to the spot where it landed and searched for his ball. But it was gone from the sand. It had rolled into the water — and caught by the surf that foamed up and ebbed back, it bobbed, a red dot floating out to sea. He barked and ran after it into the icy water, where the rough force of the waves and the pull of the undertow caught him by surprise and swept him off his feet.

"Rusty! Come back!" Jenny screamed and waved her arms wildly at him. She hesitated while he thrashed in the surf, but when a mountainous wave heaved high on the ocean, crested, and rode in toward shore, she dashed into the water and grabbed at his collar. Breakers crashed over them.

For a terrible moment, Adrianna lost sight of them. Then she saw them again. Jenny lay sprawled in the waves foaming over her. Was she stunned? Face down in the water, she didn't stir, but her hand gripped Rusty's collar as if glued there. Held by her grip, he struggled to break loose and get back on his feet as another great billow surged toward them.

Adrianna cried, "Jenny! Watch out!" But the wind tore the warning away from her lips, and it drowned in the thunderous surf. She stood, irresolute, at the water's edge, and her eyes searched the beach for help. But no one was near; Jenny's parents were far away, mere specks on the shore.

She flung her arms up at the heavy sky and screamed for help. But none came. She wavered once more, then shuddered, took a deep breath, and plunged in. The undertow ripped at her jeans and sucked at her legs, but she stayed on her feet. She reached for Jenny's hand and broke that grip on Rusty's collar. He yelped and bounded toward shore as Adrianna, panting and sobbing, dragged Jenny to dry land and fell down, exhausted, beside her.

They lay there until Jenny stirred. Coughing and sputtering, she bolted upright and peered at Adrianna through her mop of wet hair. "Oh . . . that was scary! Are you okay?"

Adrianna nodded, then looked at Jenny and burst into laughter. She giggled uncontrollably. "Oh, Jenny!" she gasped. "You look so funny! Your hair! It's all plastered down on your face."

Jenny drew herself up. "You don't look so great yourself," she said stiffly, but shoved her hair back from her face. She sat silent a moment and stared at Adrianna. Then she said, "You saved me . . . you know." She shivered and scrambled to her feet. "I'm frozen. We better dry off before my mom and dad get back."

Lips blue, teeth chattering, they trudged up the beach to the dunes. Rusty followed, his head hanging low, his coat drenched and matted. When they reached their sandy ridge, Jenny asked, "Did you bring other clothes?"

"Shorts. In my backpack."

"A shirt?"

"No."

"Let's see what's here." Jenny poked through the gear stacked near the blanket and hauled out a shirt and sweater. "Take these. They're my mom's. She always brings extra stuff to the beach."

Adrianna eyed the shirt. It was sleeveless. "No. You change into that. You're wetter than I am."

"Well . . ." Jenny turned back to the pile of clothing and dug further. She pulled out a swimsuit. "I brought this for sun-bathing," she said with a giggle. "Not exactly right for this weather. Let's see . . ." In the stack, she found her father's wind-breaker. "slip this on over my mom's shirt. It'll keep you warm. And I'll wear her sweater over my swimsuit. Okay?"

"There's no place to strip down and change." Adrianna objected. "You go ahead if you want. I'll just dry off."

"There's no one here to see us. The beach is empty. Come on — I'll do it if you will."

"No."

"Listen, I won't even look at you — if that's what's bothering you. I didn't know you were so modest."

Adrianna yielded. "Well . . . okay," she said grudgingly. "But don't look." She turned her back to Jenny and stripped off her wet sweater and jeans. She shivered and pulled on her shorts, the ones she'd intended to keep in her backpack today. She reached for the shirt.

"Hey, Addie! Your arms! And your back! They're all black and blue."

Adrianna's stomach knotted.

"You look like you backed into a brick wall. What happened?"

"You said you wouldn't look. Just finish changing." Adrianna slipped on the shirt and zipped the yellow windbreaker over it.

Jenny buttoned her mother's sweater over her swimsuit and reached for the blanket. They wrapped themselves in it as Rusty shook himself vigorously and showered them with sand.

"Rusty! You oaf!" Jenny protested. But he was gone, galloping down the beach. She turned back to Adrianna and asked, "How'd you get those bruises?"

Adrianna stared at the sky, at the mist-beaded shafts of sunlight that now streaked through the overcast sky.

"Addie!"

Trapped, and weary of her secret, Adrianna barely breathed the words, "My father hit me."

"Oh . . . Addie! Why?"

"I let Freddie break her leg."

"Oh, no . . ."

Adrianna found herself defending him. "I was wrong to let her get hurt."

"But even so . . . how could he? You're all black and blue! Did he ever . . . has he hit you before?"

Adrianna didn't trust herself to speak. She nodded.

"Listen! He can't do that! Someone has to tell him. My mom will—"

"No!"

"She'll see that he doesn't do it again. She's good at giving orders." Jenny grinned. "You know that."

Adrianna smiled ruefully at the thought of anyone giving orders to Papa. But her smile quickly faded, and she said, "Please don't tell anyone. Just forget the whole thing."

"Who else knows?"

"Mama . . . and Philomene."

"Does he hit them?"

"No."

"Not Freddie either?"

Adrianna shuddered.

"Why you?"

Tears scalded Adrianna's cheeks, and she whispered, "I don't know."

Wrapped in their blanket, they sat without talking. Then

116

Jenny said, "Are you sure you don't want my mom to call him?"

"I'm sure." Adrianna had visions of losing Jenny's friendship if Mrs. Harris told Papa what to do. She didn't think she could bear that.

They huddled in silence until Jenny said, "All right — I won't say anything."

"Thanks," Adrianna murmured. "It just wouldn't work . . ."

Jenny squinted at the sky. The sun had burned through the overcast, and they emerged from their blanket. Jenny peeled off her mother's sweater and said, "See! I told you the sun would come out. Let's soak up some sunshine. Come on, Addie — take off that windbreaker."

"But the marks . . ."

"No one'll see them. We're all alone."

They shook out the blanket and spread it on the sand, then flung themselves on it as Rusty charged back to them. He collapsed beside Jenny and stretched his paws on the blanket, resting his chin and bedraggled ears there.

Adrianna unzipped the windbreaker and tossed it aside. She basked in the sun, feeling purged of her secret and almost happy. Even her worry about Papa and Philomene — that burden seemed easier now. She dozed — and woke to find Jenny's mother laughing down at them.

"Wake up, you two! You'll sleep the day away. Aren't you hungry?" Mrs. Harris reached for the lunch basket but paused when she saw the salt-stiffened sweaters and jeans, almost dry now, spread on low clumps of ice plant. "What's this?" she asked.

"We got wet . . ." Jenny mumbled.

"How's that?" her father demanded. "We told you to stay on dry land."

"We did. But then . . ." And Jenny told their story.

Her mother sighed. "Oh, Jenny! You could have drowned. And just look at Rusty! What a sight!"

"Jenny, don't you know that Rusty could have managed without you?" her father said sternly. "Dogs have better balance than people. There really was no need to run after him."

Jenny hung her head and murmured, "Well . . . but Addie saved me."

Mrs. Harris shook her head at Jenny and started to hug Adrianna, then stopped and stared. "What are those marks?"

Adrianna's stomach knotted. She felt her face burn. She had forgotten.

Jenny spoke up quickly. "She fell and hurt herself."

"Oh — ?"

Adrianna picked up the story. "Last week . . . I got up at night to help Freddie." Jenny's mother stared long and hard as she stammered on, ". . . and I tripped . . . on her crutches."

Mrs. Harris pursed her lips. "Those marks look like someone hit you. Was it those boys? Did they hurt you again?"

"Mom!" Jenny protested. "Please! Let's eat. I'm starved."

Opening the lunch basket, Mrs. Harris laid slices of roast beef and big spoonfuls of potato salad on paper plates, but her face remained troubled. Adrianna took a thin slice of meat but shook her head at the potato salad. "I'm on a diet. I'll skip the mayonnaise."

Mrs. Harris smiled. Her face lightened, and she said, "You do look slimmer."

Adrianna smiled too. "I've lost more than twenty pounds."

"That's a lot. You could ease up now."

"Oh, no. I have a way to go yet."

While they ate, Mrs. Harris said quietly, "You didn't answer my question, Adrianna."

"Question . . . ?" Adrianna thought they had changed the subject.

Her mouth full, Jenny cried, "Mom, we told you! She fell."

Stowing his camera into its case, Mr. Harris shook his head at his wife and said mildly, "Beth, let's drop it. The girls obviously don't want to tell us."

"But — "

"I'm sure Adrianna would say if she had a problem. Those boys know better than to bother her now."

Mrs. Harris frowned, but soon her face cleared and she said, "Okay — I'll drop it. Three against one — that's too much for me."

Chapter 17

Greeted by a frenzy of noise and activity, Adrianna hesitated at the cafeteria door. She searched for Jenny and finally spotted her at a table across the room. Tim and Pete were there, Teresa too. She made her way through the commotion and joined them.

"You're late," Jenny said.

"I had to stay after class and talk to Miss Delricco about some work that I missed. I have to get it all done before spring vacation."

"That's not much time."

Adrianna nodded. She munched on a carrot stick and gazed wistfully at the food on the table. Wedges of pizza. Hamburgers in buns. French fries and soft drinks. Well, there was no point in comparing; she knew she couldn't eat things like that and lose weight. She opened her carton of yogurt while Jenny talked about their ride home from the beach last Sunday.

"We sang all the way home. And you should have heard Rusty howl. We took the coastal route. What a mistake! The curves and hills on that road — it was like a roller coaster."

"Why did you go that way?" Teresa asked. "We always go east through the valley. And then take the main highway north."

"I know. But my dad said he wanted to see the sunset on the ocean and take pictures. So he took this road that winds along the coast. And he kept starting and stopping. And Rusty got carsick. What a surprise! He never did that before."

Adrianna smiled as she recalled the ride and her relief that her own stomach had stayed quiet through all of the stopping and starting and twisting and turning on their way home.

"I don't think we'll ever go that way again. At least not with Rusty." Jenny paused for breath. "And just look at my sunburn. How's yours, Addie?"

"Not bad. Only my face really burned. But my father . . ." Embarrassed, Adrianna let her voice trail into silence as she thought about Papa's displeasure.

He had scolded her. "Common sense! Where is your common sense that you sleep in the sun?"

At the sink, Mama soaked soft cloths in vinegar and water to lay on Adrianna's face, and as she listened to Papa, Adrianna knew she could never tell him about rescuing Jenny. He would probably scold her for that too. No praise for her, ever, from him.

Lost in thought while she sat with her friends now, she was startled when Teresa said, "Wouldn't it be fun to go there together! All of us."

"Go where?" Pete asked.

"To the ocean, of course," Teresa answered. "I could ask my brother to drive. He has his license now, and my dad might let him use the station wagon. On a Saturday — if his chores are all done."

"Great!" Jenny cried. "Let's try for next weekend." She turned to Adrianna. "And you could invite Philomene. That might be nice for Terry's brother."

"Well . . ." Teresa said, "he might want to bring his own girl-friend."

"Oh . . ." Jenny looked crestfallen.

"I couldn't go," Adrianna said. "My father wouldn't let me. Or Philomene." Reflecting on their accident at the beach, she said skeptically, "But your father wouldn't let you go either — would he, Jenny?"

"Sure he would. He knows I'd never do that again."

"Do what?" Tim asked.

"Well . . ." Jenny took a deep breath. "I fell in the ocean . . .

running after Rusty. And there was a huge undertow. And Adrianna saved me."

Adrianna blushed under her sunburn as Jenny told about the rescue. "But anyway," Jenny concluded, "I think my dad will let me go. If I promise to be careful."

"How about you, Addie?" Pete asked.

She shook her head. "I don't think so. My father is really strict."

"Well, you could ask him," Tim said. "Get him in a good mood and then ask him. You never know — he might say yes."

Adrianna didn't answer, and the conversation went on without her.

✳

Later, she rode her bike home alone. Jenny had stayed at school with Gary and Miss Delricco to work on their book, but Adrianna had to hurry home and watch over Frederika. She wondered while riding her bike if after all Papa might allow her to go with her friends. She wished she had enough courage to ask his permission and perhaps even persuade him.

"Hey, Addie!" She heard a voice from behind. It was Leland — on his bike.

Her heart jumped. Her front wheel wobbled, but she straightened it and pedaled faster.

"Hey, you! Addie!" He caught up and rode alongside her.

Staring straight ahead, she lifted her head high and fastened an expression of disdain on her face. She had nothing to say to him.

"Man! Are you ever snooty!"

She clenched her teeth and concentrated on keeping her wheel steady.

Then suddenly he crowded her toward the curb. "You're so stuck-up!" he jeered. "Or maybe you're just dumb. Yeah — too dumb to talk."

Anger — unbidden, unexpected — rose up inside her, and she blurted, "Quit crowding me!"

"She talks! Fat Addie talks." Leland started to laugh and then looked appraisingly at her. "But you're not so fat anymore."

"Not so dumb either. Just because I won't talk to you — that doesn't make me dumb. And who said you could call me Addie? That name is for my friends. Not you!"

"Well, Adrianna . . ." He extended her name in a drawl. "I've got a score to settle with you. You got me in a lot of trouble." He turned his wheel sharply and braked, blocking her path.

She stopped short but kept her balance and glared at him. Her heart pounded. Her stomach churned, but she didn't retreat. "You think that was trouble? Well! You don't even know what trouble is. Start up with me again — and I'll show you trouble!" Barely raising her voice, she hissed her warning at him. But even as she uttered those brave words, she wondered where they had come from.

Leland stared at her, amazement written on his face, but he didn't move.

"Get out of my way!"

He still didn't move.

She shoved at his handlebars. Pushing his front wheel aside, she opened a path for herself and rode off.

Chapter 18

Before she went to church Sunday morning, Mama announced that she'd be gone most of the day. She planned to spend this afternoon at the meeting hall, demonstrating her special Easter pastries for the ladies at church. Adrianna promised to stay home and watch over Frederika. She didn't mind; she had homework to do.

She brought her books to the kitchen table, and while Frederika watched television with Papa, she sat down and tried to concentrate. But her thoughts wandered back to her encounter with Leland. She still felt amazed by the way she had silenced him. And very pleased. She smiled when she remembered telling Jenny about it. Jenny had hugged her and cried, "I knew you could do it!"

"It wasn't easy," Adrianna said ruefully.

"Well! Once you begin standing up for yourself, it gets easier," Jenny countered. And as they walked home from school that afternoon, they giggled all the way to their street corner. They replayed the encounter like a favorite record, with Jenny acting Leland's part and Adrianna confronting him.

In the kitchen now, Adrianna smiled again, then shook her head and focused on a story she wanted to write, one she hoped to include in the writing club's book, even though it was late. It was about her grandfather's house in Greece, with a description of the long summer days filled with pleasure that she had enjoyed there. As she started to jot her ideas down on paper, Frederika's voice from the living room distracted her. "I hate this cast, Papa. I want it off."

"The bone in your leg must heal first. Then the cast can come off." Papa sounded good-humored, and Adrianna felt a rush of relief. If he was angry at Mama for staying late at church, his voice didn't show it.

"The doctor told Mama — maybe he'll take it off on Saturday. How many days until Saturday?"

"Six."

"Then will it come off, Papa? Will it?"

"The doctor must tell us."

"I wish it was Saturday now."

"Soon it will be."

"Will you come to the doctor with me?"

"Yes."

"Six whole days . . . That's too long."

Papa's voice showed annoyance as he said, "It will pass. Look at this program now."

"I don't like it. Let's find something else."

"Leave it. I like this game show. See the prizes they give? A refrigerator. Airplane tickets. It's a good program."

"Papa . . ." Adrianna heard Philomene's voice. She had come from her room.

"What?"

"I want to talk to you."

Adrianna heard clicks from the living room, the sound of television channels being switched. Papa said, "Later, Philomene." Then he scolded Frederika. "How come you changed channels?" In the kitchen, Adrianna felt her stomach start to knot.

"I want cartoons."

"Turn back to the game show."

"Papa . . ." It was Philomene again.

"Philomene, I told you — we will talk later." He seemed more than annoyed now. He sounded angry.

Channels clicked again as Philomene said, "I want to talk now. It's about the play."

"What about it?" Papa asked, but without waiting for Philo-

126

mene's answer, he shouted at Frederika, "Turn it back! Why do you keep switching when I tell you to stop?"

"I don't like . . ."

"Put it back!"

"I want . . ."

And then he slapped Frederika. To Adrianna, it sounded like a sharp clap of thunder. She shoved her chair back and ran to the living room where Frederika lay sprawled on the floor near the television set, her crutches knocked to one side, her leg stiff and straight in its cast. Papa stood over her, his face flushed, his fists clenched.

"You hit me . . ." Frederika wailed.

Adrianna held her breath and stood, irresolute, in the doorway, but when Frederika reached for her crutches, she rushed to help. Frederika jerked away and pulled herself up, hobbling out of the room and down the hall. Soon a door slammed, and they heard a crutch banging on a bedpost, keeping time with the rhythm of her howls.

Through all the clamor, Philomene had stood without moving, her face cold and expressionless, but now she raised her voice over Frederika's outcry and said, "Papa, turn down the television. I have to ask you . . ."

"What! Why do you bother me? See how you made me hit your sister?"

"I didn't make you. You hit her for changing channels."

"What do you want?"

"You know the play . . . ?" Philomene said, her voice careful.

"I know."

"Well . . . next week we're giving two performances — one on Thursday, the other Friday."

"Sure. We'll be there on Friday."

"After the one Friday evening, the actors are going out. To a party."

Papa did not say anything. Adrianna, who stood watching,

wondered what he was thinking.

"And I want to go."

He still said nothing.

"Is it okay . . . ?"

"Who is going?"

"I told you. Everyone in the cast. The work crew too."

"How many?"

"About thirty kids."

"And grownups — what grownups?"

"Mr. Murdoch. And another teacher, Miss Temple."

"Just two grownups?"

"We don't need more. We're old enough to take care of ourselves."

Papa gave a short laugh. "Sure! Old enough for trouble."

"What kind of trouble?" There was defiance in Philomene's voice.

Without answering, he turned the television sound up, and laughter from the game show drowned Frederika's cries. Then he said over the television laughter, "This party, where will you go for it?" His tone was conciliatory — and Adrianna, observing him, thought he might yet give permission.

"I'm not sure. Someplace for supper."

"Supper? Why do you need that?"

"It's hard to eat before you go on stage."

Papa was silent.

"And after the play, everyone feels happy. And ready to eat."

"How will you pay for this supper?"

"Mr. Murdoch said we made a big profit on our ticket sales. And he said we could use some of that money for our party."

Papa stared at the screen.

"Everyone's going. I want to go too."

"And dance? Will you dance there?"

"We might."

Without taking his eyes from the screen, Papa said, "I think—

better not."

"Why not?"

"Enough that you go on the stage. To stay out late after that — and dance? The dances they do here! Better to come home."

"Please don't make me beg."

He laughed. "Who tells you to beg? Not me. I don't say you should beg."

Philomene's voice turned to ice. "Is that your last word?"

"My word? Sure, that's my word." He leaned toward the television set as if to hear better.

"Then this is mine. And you'd better listen. You don't own me. You can't always make me do what you want."

He turned to her; she had his attention now. "What did you say?" His voice was low.

"You heard me. I said you don't own me."

He stared at her. "What kind of talk is this to your father?"

"My father! What a laugh!" Philomene turned on her heel and stalked to her room.

He followed her and spoke through her bedroom door. "I tell you — come straight home after your play."

Silence from Philomene.

"You hear me?"

At last an answer came through the door. "I hear you."

"What do you say?"

"I'll come home." To Adrianna's surprise, Philomene was admitting defeat without even crying.

But Frederika still wept. Soft moans and whimpers came from that room until Papa opened her door and shut it behind him. Then the cries stopped.

Adrianna returned to the kitchen and stared at her homework. How could she concentrate now? A few minutes later, Mama bustled in and said breathlessly, "Sorry I am late."

Chapter 19

Philomene sat at supper Friday evening, but didn't eat. Stony-faced, she watched the clock and then said, "I'm going. See you later."

Adrianna reached out and touched her hand. "Good luck," she said softly.

Papa said, "Remember — we wait for you after your play."

Philomene stared at her plate.

"You hear me?"

"Yeah . . . I hear you," Philomene mumbled, her words barely audible.

After Philomene left, they ate without talking, and Adrianna picked at her food. When they finished, she stacked the dishes in the sink and Papa drove them to the high school, where he parked near the auditorium entrance, just a short distance for Frederika to hobble on her crutches.

Inside, they found four seats together. Frederika sat near the aisle, her crutches on the floor beside her. "I like this!" she said. "When will it start?"

"Not for a while," Adrianna answered.

Mama sat stiffly between Adrianna and Papa. She wore a new dress, a lavender print. She looked slimmer. And her hair looked different. What had she done to it? It seemed longer and smoother. Was she letting it grow?

"Addie!" Frederika tugged at her arm. "Look at all the people!"

Adrianna nodded. "It'll be a full house. Philomene said they sold all the tickets."

"Are my crutches in the way?"

"I don't think so."

"I don't want somebody to trip on them."

"Shh-h, Freddie. It's okay. No one will trip."

The house lights dimmed, and latecomers scurried to their seats as the curtain rose on Philomene's play. It was a light-hearted comedy filled with improbable situations — at least it seemed so to Adrianna. Frederika was enchanted, and Adrianna was, too, especially when Philomene, who looked demure and innocent in an old-fashioned costume, took off her bonnet and flirted with the leading man.

But Mama shifted in her seat, and Papa cleared his throat. In the dim light, Adrianna looked sideways at him and saw a frown on his face. He didn't seem to like Philomene's role in the play; he slouched down in his seat when the audience laughed at her. At the end of the play, the leading lady, a tall slender blonde, won out over Philomene and walked off the stage on the young man's arm while Philomene gazed longingly after them. The curtain came down to applause, and the audience called for the actors, the producer, the stage crew. The blonde girl, a bouquet of roses on one arm, held hands with the leading man, and they bowed and smiled and bowed again. When the house lights came up, Adrianna sighed, sorry it was over.

People straggled out, and the auditorium emptied while Frederika, still lost in the play, sat holding her crutches. Mama sat too. In back of them, an usher again dimmed the lights; the auditorium was dark and empty, almost cavernous.

Papa stood up and said, "Time to go. Adrianna, go find your sister. Tell her we wait."

Adrianna hurried through a side door and up a short flight of steps. She found herself backstage. It was quiet here now with no hint of activity. She saw only a man in coveralls, a janitor, who was emptying baskets of trash into a large container.

"Where is everyone?" she asked.

"Gone."

"What . . . ?"

"Yeah. They cleared out right after the play."

She stared at him.

"They'll be back tomorrow. To clean up this mess. That's not my job. I'm here to take out the trash. And lock up."

Adrianna wondered why he went on like this. "But are you sure nobody's here?" she asked hesitantly.

"See for yourself." He put his hands on his hips and jerked his head toward the scenery. "Look at that. Lots of work putting it up. More, taking it down."

As her father drove home, Adrianna tried to explain. "Papa, everyone went. Philomene would've felt silly to come home with us when everyone else was going out." She found herself running on. "They did such a good job. Don't you think they were great?"

"Be quiet," Papa said and drove on without another word.

＊

At home, Adrianna helped Frederika to bed and then wandered into the kitchen. Her mother was there, rinsing the supper dishes. Papa sat in the living room and stared at the blank television screen. His newspaper lay folded on his lap; he didn't open it. Still too restless to sleep, Adrianna sat on the couch and opened her book. She turned the pages, but the story made no sense to her.

When Mama finished the dishes, she came to the living room doorway and hesitated. Her face was troubled, but she didn't say anything to Papa, and he didn't turn to look at her. After a long moment, she sighed. "I go to sleep now," she said. "Adrianna, time now you go to bed too."

Adrianna nodded. She put her book down and went to her bed where she stared at the ceiling until she relaxed and dozed off. Waking to the slam of a car door, she heard a boy's voice. "There's a lot to clean up. We better start early."

133

She heard Philomene's answer. "Right. See you tomorrow."

Then the car drove away, and in the stillness that followed, Adrianna crept from her bed. She shivered; the night had turned chilly. Her bare feet were cold.

"Philomene!" Papa's voice came from the living room.

Adrianna stole through the hallway and hid behind the kitchen door. Frightened and worried, she peeked through the crack and saw her sister standing where Mama had stood earlier, at the entrance to the living room.

"Yes, Papa." Philomene's tone was sweet and conciliatory.

"You promised," Papa said without turning to look at her.

Philomene stood still. She didn't answer.

"You said you'd come straight home." His voice sounded sad.

"No, I didn't say that. You did. I said I'd come home, but I didn't say when." Adrianna caught her breath at her sister's insolence. She seemed to have her words well-rehearsed; she didn't even sound nervous.

"It's past one o'clock."

"I know. It got late. But wasn't the play good?"

"You lied to me."

"No, I didn't. You didn't hear me right."

Papa stayed in his chair and stared at the dark screen.

"I'm going to sleep," Philomene said. "I have to be up early." She turned away from the living room, and Adrianna could see her more clearly now.

Papa turned in his chair, and Adrianna saw his face. He looked tired and dejected. "Up early you say? And where will you go so early?"

"To knock down the scenery and put it in storage. To help the stage crew clean up."

"Tomorrow, you will stay home. I cannot trust you." His voice wasn't angry; he sounded unhappy with Philomene, disappointed that she had deceived him.

Adrianna saw Philomene walk toward him. "You can't do

this," she said. Her voice was low, and Adrianna strained to hear. "I told you — and I mean it. You can't force me. Not anymore."

"Me? I force you?" In a split second, Papa's sad tone turned to anger. "No! Not me! You're the one that forces — always crying until you get your way."

"Well, maybe I'm through with that too."

Adrianna gasped at her sister's defiance, but to her amazement Papa let it pass. Was he too tired to argue? Puzzled by their game, she fled to her room just seconds before Philomene swept through the hall and shut her door. One thing seemed clear to Adrianna; Philomene had won the argument, and Papa might not even punish her.

She heaved a sigh of relief and crawled into bed. But she felt too uneasy to sleep. She lay still and pondered about what she had heard; she didn't want to believe her suspicions.

And then she heard Papa's step in the hallway and his whisper at her sister's door. "Philomene . . ."

She heard a hiss from Philomene. "Don't come in. I told you. No more."

Adrianna heard the bedroom door open and shut. She heard Papa pleading. How could that be? What was he asking? Consumed by her need to understand, to verify that her fears and suspicions were groundless, she slipped out of bed and tiptoed to her sister's door. She pushed it open a crack. In the dark, she saw nothing, but she heard Papa say, "Just this time . . ."

"No!"

"This time . . . then no more. Tomorrow you can go to your school like you want."

"Just this time — that's what you always say! I don't believe you."

"Believe me. I promise."

It was quiet until Adrianna heard a rustle of movement. And whispers. Straining to listen, she heard her father's voice, soft and loving, with no hint of the harshness she knew in him. She heard fragments of words. "Philomene . . . so soft . . . so sweet . . ."

Adrianna's gorge rose. Her stomach crowded into her throat, and she shook with a chill that rattled her teeth. Not caring who heard, she rushed to the bathroom and switched on the light. She threw up. Long waves of nausea later, she reached for a towel. Turning, she saw her father in the doorway. He stood watching her.

"Are you sick?"

"Yes, I'm sick." She mopped at her face.

He looked at her sharply. "So — all right. Go to bed." And he went down the hall to the bedroom where Mama slept.

Chapter 20

Sunlight fell across Adrianna's bed and woke her. She glanced at the clock on her table; it was past ten. Frederika's bed was empty, the house quiet. She yawned and stretched with a lazy awareness that it was Saturday and she could sleep late. Then a feeling of horror came over her, and in a flash she remembered the awful trouble between Philomene and Papa, the disaster on which she had eavesdropped last night. She flew from her bed to her sister's door and found it open. Philomene was gone from her room. The bed was made, the spread straight and smooth, with no hint of disorder.

She stumbled into the kitchen and saw signs of breakfast — dishes in the sink, one place still set at the table. For her? She shuddered. How could she eat now? She wondered where everyone had gone until she remembered that this was the Saturday of Frederika's appointment to see if her cast could come off.

She fled to the shower and let streams of hot water pour over her head. Lifting her face, she welcomed the pulsating spray and wished she could stay here forever and wash all her terrible thoughts away. Then she sighed, turned off the water, and stepped out. She rubbed herself dry with a towel and kept rubbing until her skin stung.

She was back in her room, brushing her wet hair back from her face, when she heard the front door open and shut. She called, "Philomene . . . ?"

"Yes."

"Where were you?"

"Well! Why should I answer to you?" Philomene stood at Adrianna's open door and looked in at her.

"I was worried about you."

Philomene shrugged. "Oh, well — I went to school. We had to tear down the scenery. And pack everything away. All the props and stuff."

"Oh . . ."

"See you later. I'm tired. Got to catch up on some sleep."

"Phil . . ."

"I need a nap. I'll talk to you later."

"We have to talk now."

Philomene shifted uneasily in the doorway and said, "What is it?"

"I know."

"You know what . . . ?"

"About you and Papa." Hard words to get out, almost impossible to say.

Philomene turned pale. Her shoulders slumped, and a hand flew up to her face, covering her mouth. She came into the room and sat down on Frederika's bed. Adrianna put her arms around her, and they clung to each other without saying a word until Adrianna pulled away and whispered, "How long . . . ?" She was asking, almost begging to be told it was nothing; all a mistake, it had never happened.

"A long time."

"How could it . . . ?"

Philomene twisted her hands in her lap and looked down.

"Tell me." Adrianna waited, it seemed a long time.

When at last Philomene answered, her voice was barely a whisper. "Do you remember when we were little — and I cried to get my own way?"

"Yes."

"And sometimes I cried until Papa came . . ."

Adrianna nodded.

"Well . . . then he'd hold me and comfort me. And tell me to stop crying. And I'd kiss his cheek and say I was sorry . . ."

138

Adrianna looked away.

"Then sometimes . . . just sometimes . . . he'd let me have what I wanted." Philomene hesitated, took a deep breath, and went on. "Once in a while . . . when he kissed me, he'd stroke my face and rub my back. In a gentle way. It felt good. And afterwards, he'd let me have my way." She sighed; the sound racked her body like an old woman's cough. "That's how it started. I didn't mean anything by it. I guess he didn't either."

"And then?"

Philomene blushed. "One time he did other things too. I was surprised. I didn't understand what was happening. And he got embarrassed. He got up . . . and went out of my room."

"Where was Mama? Where was I?"

"I don't know. It was a Sunday morning. Maybe you were in church. I never liked going there." A bleak smile passed briefly over Philomene's face. She seemed lost in remembering, but then roused herself and said, "Mama wasn't even pregnant with Freddie then. It was before we went back to Greece."

"Oh . . ."

"It stopped after our trip. He didn't come in anymore . . . not for a long time. Not till after Freddie was born."

The thought flashed through Adrianna's mind that if only they had remained in Greece after that visit, perhaps this disaster would never have happened. And then she thought about Freddie. She remembered how Papa had hit her last Sunday, and how Freddie had cried on and on, and how he had gone in to be with her. A feeling of terror came over her. And disbelief. No! He wouldn't do that to Freddie. Or would he? She shook her head and tried to refocus on Philomene. "But how did it ever get started again?"

"The same way."

"But . . ."

"It was my fault. I always tried to get my way — and that's how it happened again. I think it was when a girl in school —

139

someone I liked for a friend — invited me to her house for a weekend. Yeah . . . that's how it was. And he said I couldn't go."

"And you cried?"

"Yeah . . . I cried."

"And he came in?"

Philomene nodded.

"And Mama . . . ?"

"She was with Freddie. Freddie was just a baby then . . . and she had colic . . . and cried a lot. Remember . . . her crib was in their bedroom, and Mama was always holding her and rocking her. And when Freddie would finally fall asleep, Mama would go to sleep too. Don't you remember?"

"No . . ."

"Well, that's how it was. And that night I was in my room, crying too . . . because of this girl. I really wished I could spend the night at her house and be her best friend. You know how sixth grade girls are."

Adrianna knew.

"So that night . . . when Freddie stopped crying, I just kept on. Papa came in and told me to be quiet. He told me he was sorry, but it was for my own good. He said I was at an age when boys would be after me. My friend — this girl who I liked — she had an older brother. And Papa told me I couldn't stay there all night, no matter what. So I kept on crying." Philomene shuddered. "I was curled up on my bed. And the next thing I knew . . . he was there with me. He lay down and put his arms around me . . . and it felt good. He held me . . . and stroked me . . . and soothed me . . . like petting our cat. You know, the gray one, Misty, that got lost when we went to Greece."

Tears welled up in Adrianna's eyes. For the lost cat? For Philomene? She brushed them away and stared at her sister.

"And that's how it started again." Philomene broke off her story. "You asked. So I told you."

Snatches of sex-education films flashed through Adrianna's

head. "Did he ever . . . you know . . . go in you?"

Philomene's face flamed. She nodded and hung her head. "He said he'd never hurt me," she said softly. "And he didn't. He was always gentle. Not like when he hit you."

"Hit me . . . Yes, he hit me."

"Well, he didn't hit me. And I got what I wanted. And he talked to me when we were together. He told me how much he loved me. And how he had no sons . . . and I was his only pleasure. And how Mama had turned fat and ugly."

"But where was she?"

"Asleep most of the time." Philomene's voice turned bitter. "You know, those times when he hit you . . . she tried to stop him. But she never tried to stop him from coming to me. She never tried to protect me."

"She didn't know."

"She didn't want to know. She closed her eyes and went to sleep." Philomene gave a short, bitter laugh, and tears flooded her eyes. She pushed her hair back from her face and sobbed. "Oh, Addie . . . what'll I do? Last night he said he understands that I need to be with other kids. Boys too. And he'll let me . . . but he wanted one more time. So I let him. Then he said how he was always gentle . . . and made me feel good too. And he said that no boys would be gentle like he is . . ."

They sat together, quiet now, all energy spent. Yet uneasiness stirred in Adrianna. "Phil . . ." she whispered, "you know . . . last Sunday, when you asked him about your party . . . and he said you couldn't go . . ."

"Yes."

"And he didn't go in your room . . ."

"I was glad. I just want him to leave me alone."

"But what will happen to Freddie?"

Philomene stared blankly at Adrianna.

"Last Sunday . . ."

"Yes?"

141

"He was with her."

"Oh . . ."

They clung to each other until Adrianna said, "We need help."

"I'm scared."

"So am I. I'm calling Jenny's parents."

"No, don't!" Philomene cried.

"But you just said you want him to stop."

"I do. And he said he would."

"And then what? What about Freddie?"

"He wouldn't! Not to Freddie!"

"He might." Adrianna seized Philomene's arm and shook it. "Stop crying! Go wash your face. I'm going to call."

Her resolve weakened as she dialed, and she almost hung up, but she counted the rings and held on. When Jenny finally answered, Adrianna tried to keep her voice steady.

"Jenny . . ."

"Hey, Addie!" Jenny cried. "Am I ever glad you called! Listen, it's all arranged. And I bet your father will let you come too."

"What?"

"I asked my dad about going to the beach with Teresa and her brother. And he said okay . . . as long as Teresa's mom or dad goes with us. And Teresa asked her dad, and he said he would . . ." Jenny's voice trailed off. "Addie — are you still there?"

"I'm here, Jenny. I'm in trouble . . . Philomene too . . . We need help."

Jenny's voice came through again, strong and clear. "Hold on. I'll get my dad."

Adrianna gripped the phone and waited. After a silence that seemed endless, she heard the words, "Adrianna — Jenny said . . ." It was Mr. Harris.

She interrupted him. "Please, Mr. Harris — we need to see you . . . Philomene and me. Right now." She knew the words made no sense, but there was no way to say any of this over the phone. Who would believe her?

"I'm coming," Mr. Harris said. "I'll be right there."

"Not here! Please! Meet us at Alta and Oak. Jenny knows where. She'll show you the street corner."

"We'll be there."

Adrianna slammed the phone down and called out, "Come on, Phil! We're going to Jenny's house."

She ran — and Philomene followed — out of the house and to the street corner at Alta and Oak. They saw the red Datsun; it was waiting there, its motor running. They opened the car door and jumped in.

※

Later, they told their story at Jenny's house. Adrianna sat on the couch beside Philomene and held her hand. Jenny sat facing them. Her face grim, Mrs. Harris listened while her husband asked questions. He sighed and then said, "You know, I have to tell the police."

Philomene's face went white. "Oh, no . . ." she blurted, "you can't! I should never have come here."

"Philomene," Mr. Harris said gently, "I know that you don't want to make trouble for your father."

"He never hurt me," she said through her tears. "It's just . . . I don't want to do that with him anymore."

Mr. Harris studied her face and said, "You know — much as most fathers love their daughters, we don't go to bed with them. It's not that kind of love." His glance shifted to Jenny and lingered there for a moment until he gave his head a quick shake and said, "It was wrong of him to do that."

"It was my fault too." Philomene hung her head.

"The police . . . what will they do?" Adrianna asked.

"They'll talk to you — and ask some questions."

"And then . . ."

"They'll go to your house and talk to your father."

"Is that all . . ." Adrianna insisted, "just talk to him . . . and tell him to stop?"

"Maybe not. They could arrest him. It's possible."

"I don't want him arrested," Philomene cried. "I just want him to leave me alone."

"We don't have a choice," Mr. Harris said quietly. "What your father did is a crime. He broke the law. I'd be breaking the law, too, if I didn't report it."

Philomene buried her head in her hands and whispered, "Oh, my God!"

"It's not only you, Philomene. It's your sisters too. They need protection. We've wondered about Adrianna. And now we know. He beat her so hard . . . she turned black and blue. Well . . . that's abuse too."

"I didn't tell!" Jenny said quietly to Adrianna. "They guessed."

"I know."

"We want you both to stay here with us," Mrs. Harris said. "You'll be safe here."

"I think Philomene has to . . . but I can't," Adrianna said slowly, reluctantly. "I have to go home. I can't let the police just show up there without warning. I have to tell them."

"What if he hits you?" Jenny asked.

"I don't think he will."

"I'll go with you," Mr. Harris said. "And after you talk to him, I'll bring you back here."

✳

When they pulled into the driveway and parked next to the white Cadillac, Adrianna said, "Please don't come in. I have to do this myself."

He looked at her searchingly and said, "All right. I'll wait here. Call out if you need me."

She climbed out of the car and hesitated at the front door. A shiver went through her, but she gathered her courage and went in. Frederika greeted her. "Look, Addie! My cast is off. My leg is all better."

In the kitchen, Mama turned from the sink. "Are you hungry? I save you some lunch. You know where Philomene is?"

Papa looked up from his place at the table. "That Philomene. Late again."

"I don't want anything to eat, Mama. I was at Jenny's house. That's where Philomene is."

"What is she doing there?" Papa blustered.

Adrianna looked at Frederika. "Go outside and play, Freddie. In the backyard."

"Why?" Frederika demanded.

"I need to talk to Papa and Mama alone."

"I want to stay."

Mama studied Adrianna's face and said sharply, "Go play now, Frederika. But be careful. No climbing trees."

They waited until Frederika, still complaining, went out, and then Adrianna said, "Mama, forget the dishes. Come and sit down. Papa, I must tell you . . ." Her voice faltered, but she took a deep breath and started over. "Mr. Harris is parked in our driveway. He'll come if I call him. But I need to tell you . . ."

Mama's eyes questioned her. Adrianna felt the question like a knife, a sharp pain in her stomach. "He says he must call the police," she said quietly and held off the pain, trying to ignore it.

Papa looked at her. "Police . . ."

"But I didn't want anyone to surprise you. So I came."

"Why . . . ?" Mama said slowly.

Adrianna looked down at her hands. "I talked to Philomene today. She told me." She watched her father from the corner of her eye and saw his face blanch. She reached across the table and touched his hand. "Mr. Harris has to report what you did."

"What he did . . . ?" Mama said. "What? He hit you . . . ?"

"Well, that. Yes, he hit me. He beat me. Papa, you had no right . . ."

"But I said the next day . . . I said I was sorry." Papa looked old. His bluster was gone.

"I know . . ." Adrianna remembered her feeling of love when he said he was sorry and brought home the typewriter to comfort her. "But Papa . . . you can't make up for some things just by saying you're sorry."

He stared at her, his eyes blank.

"And Philomene . . ." Adrianna said, "how can you make up for what you did to her?" She stopped. There wasn't a sound in the room; she felt she was drowning in silence. She took a deep breath and went on. "You treated her like . . . a grownup. And she wasn't. She was only a child."

"No!" He denied it. "Not like a grownup. I never hurt her. I was always careful."

"Careful! Papa! What are you saying?"

He fell silent.

"And Freddie. How about her?"

"Frederika!" He reared up, his eyes on fire. "I never touched her."

"You hit her."

"Once. I hit her one time. Nothing more."

Mama, her eyes filled with pain, looked from Papa to Adrianna. There was knowledge, centuries old, in her eyes.

Adrianna felt centuries old too. "Anyway, I had to tell you. I couldn't let some stranger come here and surprise you. Mr. Harris has to call the police, and they'll come and talk to you. I'm going back to Jenny's house now."

Chapter 21

Adrianna sat on a bench in the courthouse corridor and waited to testify. Jenny's mother sat with her. Weeks of investigation had passed, and now here they were. Mrs. Harris reached for her hand and said softly, "Let's go in. They'll be calling you soon. We can sit in the courtroom and wait."

Adrianna shuddered. "What will I say when they call me?"

"Tell the truth. Tell what you know."

Pulling the heavy door open, Adrianna hesitated there, surprised by how small the courtroom was. The section for spectators was empty — except for one person, a woman, the social worker who had come to see them after Mr. Harris called the police. Sitting in the front row of seats just back of the railing, she turned and nodded when they entered, but her face remained serious, unsmiling and guarded. They slid into seats beside her.

Adrianna saw Mama and Philomene. They sat at a table in front of the railing, and a man was with them, a lawyer from the district attorney's office. Papa sat at another table with his attorney. The judge faced them. He sat high on his bench, and everyone looked up when they spoke to him. Below that bench was a woman who tapped busily on a little machine. Her fingers flew as she recorded every word spoken by the man who was testifying. Adrianna recognized him; he was the police officer who had come and talked to them that terrible day when they fled to Jenny's house.

"Adrianna Espirikos!"

It was her turn. Someone opened a gate in the railing and showed her where to sit. She felt like a sleepwalker. When the judge asked if she knew how serious the charges were, her throat constricted. But she nodded and whispered, "Yes." Then she told him her story.

He listened and asked questions. The lawyers didn't bother her much. Papa's lawyer asked about the nice things that Papa brought home, and the district attorney asked about the times when he hit her. As she answered those questions, she looked hard at her father, but he stared at the table without meeting her eyes.

When she finished, she returned to her seat beside Mrs. Harris. Then her mother testified. And Philomene too. But Adrianna hardly heard what they said. She tried to listen when the judge questioned her father, but it knotted her stomach to see him behaving like a small boy who knew he'd been bad and now feared the punishment about to follow. Adrianna closed her ears to that testimony. It was too painful.

After everyone testified, Papa's lawyer asked the judge for probation. The prosecutor whispered to the social worker and then said, "Your Honor, we're not interested in sending this man to prison. There is the issue of protecting the family. But we're also concerned about financial support and psychiatric treatment."

The judge nodded. He spoke about the gravity of Papa's offense. But he said there were many considerations, and it would take him some time to reach a decision. He warned Papa to stay away from the house, and he ordered them all to return for his ruling a week from this day.

✳

It was Saturday afternoon at home, and Adrianna sat with Frederika on the couch in the living room. The television set was dark, and in the unnatural quiet Adrianna turned the worn pages of an old book of fairy tales and read aloud to her sister. While she read, she thought about the judge and Papa and the court hearing. Her thoughts wandered far from the story, and she faltered at times, but when she said a word wrong, her sister corrected her. It was the story of Rumpelstiltskin, and Frederika knew it by heart. Stumbling along, Adrianna stopped in mid-sentence and caught her breath at the sound of a car pulling into their driveway. Her mother came from the kitchen, and they exchanged glances.

"Is it Philomene — do you think?" Mama asked.

Adrianna shook her head. "No, Mama. She told me . . . last week . . . when she and Mrs. Harris came for her clothes. She said she wouldn't be back. She made me promise . . . if she calls, I'm to bring what she needs to Jenny's house." Adrianna's voice faltered. She felt guilty — as if she were betraying her mother by helping Philomene.

A key turned in the front door, locked and bolted now. A heavy hand turned the knob, but the bolt — installed last week by Mama and Adrianna — held the door shut. Adrianna whispered, "It's Papa."

Mama nodded, and her face drained of color.

"Papa! It's Papa!" Frederika cried. She jumped up from the couch and ran to the door.

They heard Papa's rough voice. "It's me."

Straightening her shoulders, Mama walked slowly to the door, slid the bolt clear, and opened it. Papa stood there, a suitcase in one hand, a bulky paper sack in the other. He stared at her. "What is this — a bolt on the door?"

Mama didn't answer. Instead she said, "Why you are here?"

"I need some clothes. For the warm weather. And some tools from the garage."

Frederika danced around her father. "Did you bring me something?"

A smile eased the lines of his face. "A coloring book." He set down his suitcase and reached into the paper sack, offering her a book and a new box of crayons.

149

Frederika held out her hand, then looked at her mother. "Can I . . . please?"

"All right. Take it. And go to the kitchen. You can color there." To her husband, Mama said, "Come in. And get what you need."

Leaving the door ajar, they trailed into the house, and without another word, Papa walked slowly, heavily, down the hallway to their bedroom. Adrianna turned to look at her mother who sat down on the couch and stared at her hands, the fingers tightly interlaced in her lap.

It seemed just moments later when he returned and stood at the doorway to the living room. He set his suitcase down beside him. "I got some clothes. The tools I need — I'll get them from the garage."

Mama nodded.

"I'll go now," he said. Yet he stood.

Adrianna studied his face as he hesitated. He looked tired. And old. And grief-stricken. She felt her heart constrict. What had she done to him?

As though reading her thoughts, he said, "Why you do this, Adrianna?" His voice wasn't rough. It was sad.

"Do what?" Mama said.

"Call the police." Papa's voice shook.

Silence hung heavy between them, and tears slid down Adrianna's cheeks. Finally she whispered, "But would you have stopped if I didn't?"

Papa jerked his head back as if she had slapped him. He stared at her in silence, then picked up his suitcase and left. Adrianna stood frozen while sounds of him rummaging for tools came from the garage. Finally, a car door slammed, and the Cadillac backed slowly out of the driveway.

He did not come back to the house after that, and it was not until the next week at the court hearing that Adrianna saw him again. At the hearing, Papa stood, his head bowed, while the judge announced his ruling. He rebuked Papa for having gone to the house and ordered him to stay away unless he called first for Mama's permission. The judge looked at Mama when he said this, and she nodded. Then he imposed a requirement of counseling and court supervision for everyone in the family. This time, the social worker nodded, and the attorneys agreed that it was the best way. Before he dismissed them, the judge warned Papa that if through poor judgment or some foolish mistake he should violate the terms of his probation, it would all be revoked and he would go to prison.

Chapter 22

Through the weeks that followed, Adrianna tried to get used to the way things were at home now — living there with only Mama and Frederika. It seemed so quiet, and so strange. And in school, while she tried to concentrate on her work, she thought about all the changes. How would their life be if she had not called Mr. Harris that day? She didn't know. She only knew that she had ruined her father's life. And Mama's.

She felt ashamed and guilty, and at school when Mrs. Feldman sent for her, she hesitated at the office door and wondered if anyone in the school office knew about Papa and the judge and his ruling. As she stood there, Mrs. Feldman looked up from the papers on her desk and said, "Come in. My, you look slim."

Adrianna nodded. She came in and sat on a chair, the one she had occupied months ago when her parents came with her to complain about Leland.

"I asked Miss Delricco to excuse you from class. So we could talk," Mrs. Feldman explained.

Adrianna wiped the palms of her hands on her skirt and said tentatively, "I haven't missed school any days . . ."

"It's not that. A social worker from the court called me."

"Oh . . ." So Mrs. Feldman knew about Papa.

"She told me that your father is on probation."

Adrianna winced.

"And your sister is living away from home."

"Yes . . . with my friend, Jenny, and her parents."

"And you're still at home . . ."

"Yes."

"She — this probation worker — asked me to keep in touch with you . . ."

"Oh . . . ?" Adrianna looked questioningly at Mrs. Feldman.

"So I can contact her if you have trouble with your father."

Adrianna shook her head. "I could call her myself. I have her number."

"But would you?"

Not sure of her answer to that, Adrianna looked down and said nothing.

"Adrianna," Mrs. Feldman said gently, "do you understand all the terms of your father's probation? That's your best protection. That, and calling her if you have trouble."

"I think I understand."

"Good. You know he has to support the family."

"Of course." Adrianna knew Papa would support them. He always had.

"And he has to stay away from your home . . ."

This was the part that hurt Adrianna, the part she knew was her fault. She sat silent.

Mrs. Feldman was silent, too, until with what seemed like an effort, she asked, "How is your sister?"

"Philomene . . . ? Okay I guess. I don't see her a lot. But we talk on the phone."

"And you? How are things for you?"

"Not so good." Adrianna's eyes filled with tears.

"Tell me."

Adrianna felt almost impatient with Mrs. Feldman and her questions. She said slowly, unwillingly, "I feel terrible about what I did."

"But it's not your fault. You had to . . ."

"It's hard to think so when I see my mother cry."

Mrs. Feldman shook her head. "You know . . . your mother needs help with this . . . It must be so hard for her. Is she in therapy?"

"We all are. Even Freddie." Adrianna smiled ruefully through her tears. "She's in play therapy."

"And you see someone?"

"Well, me . . . I go once a week and talk to a social worker — Mr. Linn."

"How about your father?"

"He lives across town. But we see him on Thursdays — in family counseling."

"Does he go for individual therapy?"

"He has to. He sees a psychiatrist . . . and a probation officer. That's what the judge ordered . . ." Adrianna's voice trembled as she recalled the judge's stern warning to Papa and the sudden small jerk of her father's head as he nodded agreement.

And in her own head now, she heard once again the echo of his lawyer's words, "Your Honor, we do understand — and we thank you for your clemency." Lost in remembering, Adrianna saw and heard it all over again like a bad dream she could never forget, a paradox of a nightmare with blurred edges sharply etched in her memory forever.

She stirred. "I have to go now."

"Wait a minute. Tell me how school is going."

"Well . . . I have trouble concentrating. Especially in math and science. But I'm trying."

"Any trouble with Leland?"

"No. Nothing there." Adrianna recalled Papa's indignation and anger at Leland. And the new bike he brought home to comfort her. She sighed.

Mrs. Feldman sighed, too, and said softly, "Things will get better, Adrianna. It's hard to think so now. But believe me . . ."

Adrianna didn't trust herself to speak. She shook her head and went back to class.

✳

155

The school day passed like a dream, its happenings unreal, and after school she rode her bike to her meeting with Mr. Linn. Keeping her company, Jenny rode with her. They pedaled without talking until Jenny said, "You know, our book is finished. And printed."

"I know. Gary gave me a copy."

"I wish we had one of your poems in it."

Adrianna shook her head. "After I missed all those meetings . . ." Her voice trailed off. Her mind was on other things. "Jenny, do you think the kids at school have heard about my father?"

"I don't think so. No one's said anything to me."

"Mrs. Feldman knows."

"That's different. I don't think anyone else does."

They rode without talking until they came to a wood-shingled house, an old residence turned into offices, where Adrianna met each Tuesday with Mr. Linn. Turning her bike, Jenny said, "See you tomorrow. Any message for Philomene?"

"Just my love." But as Jenny started off, Adrianna called after her, "Tell her Mama's taking English lessons. In a class — at night school. And tell her I'll see her Thursday."

In the waiting room, Adrianna sat and leafed through a magazine until Mr. Linn came for her. Then they walked down a long hallway to the back of the house, to the small cluttered room that was his office.

She talked. He sat slumped in a chair, listening and studying her face, while she talked about the last courtroom session. "The judge . . . he treated my father like a criminal who couldn't be trusted . . . or . . . like . . . someone who's more of a child than a grownup."

"Maybe in some ways, he isn't a grownup."

Adrianna stared at Mr. Linn. How could that be?

"Your father worked hard when he came to this country and struggled to start his business."

"Yes . . ."

"And he succeeded . . ."

Reflecting on the house and the Cadillac and the presents, she nodded.

"That makes him seem like a strong adult. But think about his actions. Are they really the actions of someone who has grown up?"

She listened and wondered about that. Soon Mr. Linn resumed his silence, and Adrianna tried to find words for her thoughts. It seemed strange to think about Papa as not being strong and secure, sometimes too rough, but always sure of himself. Yet she asked herself now — how could he have acted that way and kept such a secret with Philomene? Surely no real adult ever would.

And what about his rages, the storms of anger when he beat her? Remembering those rages now, she was swept by a torrent of her own anger at him. He had seemed so powerful. And she had accepted his harsh discipline as his right, a prerogative that came with his strength and authority. Now she was beginning to feel that he wasn't strong at all. He was just a terribly confused person who concealed his own awful weakness behind a mask of authority. Yet through her outrage, she felt a stirring of love for him. "I miss him," she said sadly, ". . . and Philomene."

Philomene. Adrianna wondered what Philomene said to Mr. Linn in her own sessions with him. Did she acknowledge that in the end — and at last — Mama had protected her by bringing charges against Papa? Did she admit that Mama's eyes were no longer closed and she wasn't asleep anymore? Adrianna didn't ask.

The hour was almost up, but Adrianna kept talking. She asked Mr. Linn about the nausea that so often swept over her. Was it fear and tension that had knotted her stomach and sent those waves upward?

He nodded.

Fear of what? Of Papa's anger at her? Of the secret between him and Philomene?

157

He studied her face and nodded again.

Her mind in turmoil, Adrianna was silent as she tried to sort out her thoughts and emotions, her hopes and fears. Could it be that by seeing her father as he really was and giving up her fear of him, she might also lessen her other troubles?

Mr. Linn rose from his chair. "Our time is up," he said gently. "We'll talk more about this when you come back next week."

Adrianna shook her head in bewilderment. How could she hope to understand it all?

He walked to the door with her and said, "It's a slow sorting-out process. But we'll keep on working. And I'll see you Thursday with the rest of the family."

She left with mixed feelings. She was puzzled and confused. But through her confusion, she felt a stirring of belief that she would somehow — through all of this talking with Mr. Linn — find a new way to feel about her father. And about herself.

Chapter 24

Next Thursday, when Adrianna rode her bike from school to Mr. Linn's office, she saw her mother waiting in the shade of an old gnarled oak tree that grew by the wood-shingled house. As Adrianna drew near, it struck her that her mother looked good, younger even, more like the young woman in the snapshot that hung in the hallway at home, the picture of her and Papa in Greece before they were married. Seeing her now, Adrianna thought that her mother still looked stocky, but not fat anymore. And her hair, no longer frizzed, framed her face in its own natural curl. Pleased, she wondered how, in their day-to-day life at home, she could have missed seeing these changes.

She parked her bike, kissed Mama's cheek, and sat down on the broad wooden steps at the entrance. Her mother sat with her and asked, "How was school today?"

"All right. I got all my work done."

They sat without talking until Philomene came. She sighed and dropped her books on the steps, then settled herself beside Adrianna and said, "Finals next week. I'm loaded with homework."

Mama reached across Adrianna and patted Philomene's hand. "You look skinny."

"I'm okay."

"You eat good now?"

"Pretty good."

". . . and sleep?"

Philomene sighed. "No . . . There's a lot that I'm trying to get straight in my head. At night I do a lot of thinking."

"Maybe you come home soon?"

"No, Mama."

"No . . . ?"

"We can talk about it with Mr. Linn. But things are better for me where I am. And Mr. Harris said that when I'm a senior next year, he'll help me look for a scholarship. To college. Or nursing school. I'd like that."

Just then Papa drove up and parked his car at the curb. He stepped out and walked to the steps. Tentatively, he reached out to Mama and touched her hand; she didn't pull away.

"How are you?" he asked.

"Me . . . ?" She seemed surprised at his question and answered slowly. "Better now — I think."

"Your hair, I like it this way."

Mama blushed.

"Frederika, how is she?"

"All right. But some nights she cries."

"Oh . . ."

"She wants you should come home."

Tears glistened in Papa's eyes. Adrianna had never seen tears there before. "I want it too," he murmured. "I hope . . ." He looked at Adrianna and Philomene.

"Hello, Papa," Adrianna said.

Philomene said nothing. It was time to go in.